The
Ruthless
Realtor
Murders

Also by David A. Kaufelt

Six Months with an Older Woman
The Bradley Beach Rumba
Spare Parts
Jade (*under the name Lynn Devon*)
Late Bloomer
Midnight Movies
The Wine and the Music
Silver Rose
Souvenir
The Best Table (*under the name Richard Devon*)
American Tropic*
The Fat Boy Murders*
The Winter Women Murders*

*Published by POCKET BOOKS

The Ruthless Realtor Murders

A Wyn Lewis Mystery

David A. Kaufelt

POCKET BOOKS

New York   London   Toronto   Sydney   Tokyo   Singapore

POCKET BOOKS, a division of Simon & Schuster Inc.
1230 Avenue of the Americas, New York, NY 10020

ISBN: 0-671-51147-5

First Pocket Books hardcover printing November 1997

10 9 8 7 6 5 4 3 2 1

For Lynn Mitsuko Kaufelt, with love.
Realtor? Yes. Ruthless? Never.

Author's Note

Waggs Neck Harbor is based on the Long Island village of Sag Harbor, though none of the characters or events or establishments herein are anything but pure invention.

I'd like to thank my friend Joan Carlson, who continues to pass on inspiring, delicious village gossip; Molly Allen, whose incisive intelligence and dry wit have helped illuminate every page of this book; and Bill Grose, who provided crucial early intervention.

I'd also like to thank the associates of Prudential Knight Realty for answering my relentless questions, with great humor, about the arcane real estate process.

Diane Cleaver, that star agent who got me to start writing the Wyn Lewis series in the first place, died last year, leaving a permanent black hole in my universe.

D.A.K.
Key West, Florida

Cast of Characters

The Ruthless Realtors

Petronella St. Cloud—The grand dragon of Southampton realty, she shows one mansion too many.

Kathy Carruthers—Determinedly down-home, she's been *the* Montauk Realtor forever and a day too many.

Wynsome Lewis—Second-generation Waggs Neck Harbor village Realtor, she knows where the bodies are—she so often finds them.

Law Enforcement

Lieutenant Detective Pasko—Tough and tightly focused, he longs to get back to the action (NY, NY) but needs a big solve to do so.

Cora—Tough and tightly focused (on Pasko), she's the computer conduit to the national as well as the local crime scene.

Homer Price—Waggs Neck Harbor's first black police

chief, he's ordered to work with Pasko but has his own ideas about who the killer is.

Ray Cardinal—Red-headed and raw, he's recently been promoted to sergeant by his idol, Homer Price.

Captain Savage—His métier is making life difficult for Pasko.

Major Players

Frank and Merredith Jones—Brother and sister developers, they specialize in redoing old village houses, making lots of money and enemies in the process.

Mike Bell—Muscle-bound and surly, he feels his family has been done out of their due and he's going to get even, no matter what it takes.

LeRoy Stein—Son of a local heiress and a European D.P.; among the three of them they managed to lose their silk shirts in real estate ventures.

Lettitia (Lettie) Browne—Oft-retired actress and proprietor of the local inn, she's doing what she can for Mike Bell.

Liz Lum—Wyn's erstwhile assistant; her daughter—Heidi—is also doing what she can for Mike Bell.

Tommy Handwerk—Carpenter, village heartthrob, and Wyn Lewis's husband, now he wants to be a dad.

Nick Meyer—Wyn's ex-husband; he and his zillionaire mother continue to include her in family goings-on.

Some Dead People
Who Intrude on the Present

Penny McFee and Harriet Leverage—A pair of attorneys killed a decade ago in a manner remarkably similar to current practices.

Myra Fiske Stein—LeRoy's much loved mom, she was a village princess who married the wrong man.

Roman Stein—An outsider who thought he'd make a killing in Eastern Long Island real estate.

Flinty Jones—Bereft widower and father of Frank and Merredith, he made a nice living from his junkyard until he hooked up with Roman.

Some Village Folk

Antiquities shop owner Dickie ffrench
Jane Littlefield ffrench, Dickie's spouse
Lucy Littlefield, Jane's dotty aunt
Yolanda, smart-mouthed secretary to Homer Price
Mrs. Pizza, restaurant owner
Thelma Eden and her daughter, Mary Jane, of the Eden Café
Patty Batista, spa owner and aerobics animal

Prelude

Rain or shine, Petronella St. Cloud, a lean and mean seventy-six, made her daily fourteen-mile bike ride through Southampton township as if it were duck soup.

A chiropodist's daughter, she had spent the last sixty years of her life transforming herself into the doyenne of Southampton's real estate brokers. Working, as she claimed, twenty-five-hour days, flogging shacks near the lake in the beginning and then ranch houses off the highway and then gingerbreaded village houses and finally beachfront mansions, sitting on every possible charity board from Shinnecock Indian relief to the home for unwed Catholic mothers, turning every acquaintance into a contact, Petronella had laboriously, patiently achieved her goal. She was a fixture at all important society events, a near intimate of those to and for whom she sold property, every petty official's confidante. If one had any social aspirations whatsoever, one purchased one's house through Petronella St. Cloud.

Thus she had won the long, hard Realtors' War, but the greatest battle had to be, more's the pity, unsung. Mostly because it was not exactly legal.

Petronella closed her obsidian eyes against the pleasant glare of Eastern Long Island's rising spring sunshine, propped her bike against the impressive barrier wall of Duck Farm Acres, an extremely up-scale development, and allowed herself the luxury of remembering that delicious vintage real estate year, 1985.

It hadn't started well, a glut of overpriced houses on the market and a glut of unemployed and suddenly strapped Wall Street types wanting to know why. "No buyers, Stupid," were the words Petronella forced herself not to say. No income, either, and, as it happened, Petronella was then rather long on investments and short on cash.

She was so distracted she allowed herself to be elected chair of the local zoning board, figuring it would give her something to do besides fret over unsold, unsellable properties and mortgages coming due. It wouldn't have been pretty, losing face in her world, as well as properties to the banks. Her enemies would have made the most of it. Her very career—her life—would be over, and then what would become of her? The specter of the Bide-a-Wee Home for the Aged loomed large in her nightmares.

Then a queer kind of angel, a person whose name Petronella had sworn to never let pass her lips, at least in conjunction with the duck farm development, approached her with the sort of extralegal proposition she had never before considered entertaining.

It was a classic real estate scam. The last important

undeveloped acreage within the town limits was Teresa Bell's duck farm. Teresa, a tough Waggs Neck Harbor girl, had attempted to work it herself, with the help of her no-account husband, Victor Bell, and her extraordinary brood of not surprisingly no-account children. So fertile were the Bells that at one point there was a Bell in every grade of the Waggs Neck Harbor school system.

Needless to say, the Bells as managers did not work out, and a desperate Teresa leased the farm to her brother-in-law, who disappeared within six months, stripping the farm of everything but pathetic, starving ducks and the rancid, stomach-turning smell endemic to duck farms.

Petronella's informant had learned that the farm was about to be taken by the state in lieu of back taxes, that Teresa's only shot at making any sort of money was to sell it to a Riverhead duck farmer who was evincing interest.

But if Petronella took action, quickly, Teresa could be cut out. Because here was a golden opportunity for enrichment vis-à-vis a major, elitist housing development.

"But," Petronella objected, "the duck farm is undevelopable. It's grandfathered in as farmland. Virtually untouchable."

Her new business partner had said perhaps it was time that the county zoning board took a look at an industry that had been outlawed as unhealthy in virtually every other town in the state. Petronella, a quick study, said yes, it was.

Within the week the Petronella-chaired zoning board proscribed duck farming within the city limits; and Kathy Carruthers, a Realtor buddy of Petronella's, had convinced the Bells to list and sell their heavily mort-gaged land.

The buyers were an unlikely limited partnership made up of a Waggs Neck Harbor heiress, her son, and a self-made king of junk.

Ill-equipped to develop anything, the partnership went bankrupt in a matter of months, and a new com-bine—known as Duck Farm Acres, Inc., and repre-sented by Kathy Carruthers and Petronella St. Cloud, stepped into the picture.

This legal entity bought the property on the court-house steps and proceeded to develop it into a splen-did, multimillion-dollar property.

Petronella and Kathy not only collected their hefty commissions but were named members of the Duck Farm Acres board. The principal board member, how-ever, remained unidentified.

There was some noise, raised by the Bells, about the legitimacy of Petronella sitting on the zoning board that condemned a property she later helped to broker, not once but twice.

But this potential scandal was lost in the double trag-edy that occurred in Southampton Village that season. The "sort of thing that couldn't happen here" did, and the Eastern Long Island villages were shaken. Two pop-ular, well-connected young female attorneys were strangled in their offices, motive unknown, their killer never found.

They were silly girls, working unattended in their unlocked offices, Petronella told herself. And they had been only marginally connected with the duck farm sale.

And as for the Bells and the other Waggs Neck Harbor fish, she refused to feel guilty. They would have been ripped off by anyone who felt like it. Petronella and Kathy and the One Who Had to Remain Unnamed just got there first. There was nothing to feel guilty about except for a tiny bending of the laws.

But deep down in her sere little heart, Petronella knew better.

Chapter

1

DONE WITH HER MORNING EXERCISE, PETRONELLA HAD changed costume and vehicle and made herself ready to show Shadows, the oceanfront white elephant she was hoping to unload. She had received it nearly a decade before in lieu of commissions owed when the former owner went bankrupt.

The playful prospect had characteristically insisted on anonymity ("Never mind who this is") but Petronella knew. That telltale voice was a giveaway, no matter what the disguise. Shadows seemed a perfectly appropriate house and Petronella had good reason to believe this particular fish was ready to bite.

No sooner had Petronella hung up on that Friday-afternoon caller than Wynsome Lewis phoned. It never poured, Petronella thought. She had been sitting on Shadows for years and now suddenly there was interest.

Wyn had only requested a clientless preshowing,

which in Realtor practice was like foreplay without touching; but on this bright spring Saturday morning, Petronella was in what was for her a sunny mood. If *numero uno* didn't buy Shadows, then Wynsome's ex-mother-in-law, Audrey Meyer, might. The thought of a bidding war between two rich contenders made her weak with anticipation.

Wyn's ex-mother-in-law seemed the more likely purchaser, owning, as she did, the estate next to Shadows and interested in expansion. At this stage of her game Petronella St. Cloud didn't do previews, but this was all too fortuitous, so she had sniffingly agreed.

Besides, Petronella was well disposed toward Wynsome Lewis. That presumably genuine platinum hair cut in a Prince Valiant "do" suited her right down to her otherworldly silver-gray eyes.

Wyn was thirty-five if she was a day, but she exuded youth and soured goodness and an irritating poker-faced naïveté. Having worked with Wyn on a number of occasions, Petronella didn't for one minute swallow the naïveté or the goodness.

Truth be told, she rather admired the younger woman. If Petronella had been a woman given to sisterly relationships, she might have befriended Wyn.

But they had such different roles to play. Petronella was Old Southampton Village, noblesse-obliging it to the lesser souls of poor, service-oriented Waggs Neck Harbor. Wyn, determinedly democratic and intellectual, represented Waggs Neck, unimpressed by the would-be aristocrats of that superficial beach resort, Southampton. True friendship was out of the question.

In any case, Petronella was not exactly ecstatic about Wyn's progress. She had returned to the East End of Long Island a decade ago following a disastrous brief marriage and had taken over her dead father's realty business; the rest was local real estate history.

The timing had been very right. Semi-impoverished buyers, scaling down, were looking for smaller and cheaper houses, which Waggs Neck Harbor had in abundance. Still, credit had to be given where credit was due. Petronella was the first to admit that Wynsome Lewis knew her onions. She was making a fortune in commissions and reportedly socking it away against a potential down curve. She sure wasn't spending it on wardrobe, Petronella observed.

Wyn's officious mother had decamped for Manhattan and the glamour of a late-life career in higher education, trading the commodious old Lewis family house in Waggs Neck for the cramped one-bedroom, one-bath West Side co-op Wyn had received in her divorce settlement. It was all too neat for Petronella, who didn't trust convenient solutions.

Her latest assistant had still not arrived by the time Petronella had to leave. She scratched an indecipherable, rancorous note, locked up, got into her behemoth of a car, and, damning the chirping birds overhead who were giving her a headache, took off.

When Petronella reached Shadows, she had to get out and push open the David Selznick gates. The lock had rusted and fallen apart some time ago. As she got back behind the oversized steering wheel, she glimpsed a large automobile parked in the driveway of Audrey Meyer's neighboring estate.

Either the prospect was in the wrong drive or, worse thought, well-to-do day-trippers, already emerging from winter hibernation (it was only late April, for God's sake), were enjoying a self-guided tour of the mansions of Southampton. She'd have to call the police, she told herself, suspecting the latter.

The drive up to Shadows had been cleverly planned to maximize the length of the property, long rather than wide with lots of unanticipated curves and surprising berms, the roadside overgrown and atmospheric. But no real land, Petronella reminded herself, scanning her property with her infamous gimlet eye. Less than three acres. And at the wrongish end of Lily Pond Lane. Perhaps this would be her lucky day and she could unload Shadows. She crossed her fingers.

The fish hadn't arrived yet—no car was to be seen—so Petronella parked her ancient La Salle on the far side of the semicircular driveway, inhaled a thin chestful of ocean air—which she wrongly believed beneficial for her neuralgia—opened the front door, and walked across the ill-proportioned rotunda of a foyer.

She had intended for some weeks to disengage the outrageously expensive battery-operated alarm system the blood-sucking insurance people had insisted upon even though Shadows was uninhabited. This seemed as good a time as any. The mechanism was secreted under the central staircase.

And so was the fish.

Chapter

2

It was a seasonable Eastern Long Island spring day, the sun a convincing yellow, a muted breeze coming off the gray-green ocean, white-capped waves a surfer's dream.

Wynsome Lewis was driving along, singing a favorite song ("I'm Just a Prisoner of Love") with a 1937 Bing Crosby on the tape deck, knowing she should be feeling put out, her ex-mother-in-law's unreasonable demands usually a just cause for a case of the pity-me's.

Not today, even though it was early on a Saturday morning and she had to pry herself away from bed and the embrace of her all-American toy boy of a husband and her aging yellow Lab, Probity, who had been a bad, bad girl on the linoleum kitchen floor.

Should have left it for Tommy to clean up, she told herself, but she was feeling uncharacteristically generous and even nice this morning, two emotions against her usual grain. Having lowered the ragtop on her beloved old Jaguar, glorying in the first real spring day of the season, Wyn told herself she'd better chill before she broke into the score from *The Sound of Music* and people mistook her for a rhapsodic nun.

Still, she couldn't keep the buoyancy down, even with Petronella St. Cloud waiting for her. Her favorite flowers, white lilacs, were in bloom all over the South Fork and the resultant ambrosial aroma combined with the salt spray were enough to make her believe in aromatherapy.

She finally put a lid on the bubbling happiness pot when she maneuvered her car through Shadows's wide-open gates and drove up the long, unnecessarily sinuous, and potholed drive. Instead of lilacs, here late April weeds were in full flower and Shadows's languid air of doom was definitely dampening.

The thought of Tommy brought another tiny burst of joy—a reminder of how much she loved him. She wondered yet again at the depth of this emotion, still amazed at having chosen not only a certified male beauty, but a fellow who was unarguably a good, moral, ethical person without, as they said in England, side. Many of her friends neither liked nor understood their relationship, feeling Wyn had stepped down a rung. She didn't much care.

Daunted by the cracked stones of Shadows's once elaborate pathway, cursing herself for wearing the inappropriate low red heels just because they were new, Wyn stopped for a moment to look at the house.

The brick needed serious repointing; the half dozen chimneys were falling down; the barrel-tiled roof was due for total replacement. Shadows, she concluded sadly, was a tear-down. Wyn tried for a detached cynicism, but tended to get sentimental over old houses.

Shadows had once been an imitation English country

house, built before the big wars, when Southampton was a rich second-generation Irish resort, long before it was discovered by the post-World War II moneyed international set.

It was an irony Wyn tried not to savor that Petronella, the foot doctor's daughter (oh, everyone knew), had been saddled with Shadows when the aristocratic Myra Fiske Stein had lost it along with everything else.

Wyn, of course, knew exactly how much the property was worth, and so, of course, did Petronella. Both Realtors also had a fair idea of how much Wyn's ex-mother-in-law was willing to pay for it.

Over the phone Petronella had claimed that there was a great deal of interest in Shadows. Wyn said ha! and observed that Petronella would be doing her heirs a favor if she could unload it. The new rich weren't interested in the Hamptons. They were headed for Litchfield County, Connecticut, and homey, pricey rusticity.

"That's how much you know, Wynsome," Petronella said. "I am showing Shadows to an extremely hungry fish early on Saturday morning. You may come right after, if you must, but you do know that I don't enjoy idle previews."

Wyn also knew that Petronella was subscribing to that hoary ploy of having prospective buyers overlap. If there was any real interest, sparks of envy might fly and ignite a bidding war resulting in an actual sale. Wyn was aware that there wasn't much that Petro didn't know about the dark side of real estate transaction.

A mean thought came to her: Was she turning into a Petronella St. Cloud, the kind of career "gal" who lived for no other thought than profit and mercantile self-advancement? No, Wyn told herself, not quite certain. Tommy's love and tons of money would save her.

She walked around Petro's vintage sedan, thinking it looked like the vehicle Gloria Swanson swanned around in during *Sunset Boulevard*. She wondered where the potential client's car was and supposed that they had met at Petronella's office and that Petro had driven them here—though she usually preferred using her clients' gasoline.

Stop being bitchy about Petro, Wyn told herself. Petronella had her quirks but she was a strong woman who had braved the realty world when it belonged to devil man, and she had conquered it all by herself. She should be a heroine of the woman's movement, except she doesn't believe in it and neither do I, Wyn admitted to herself, not being very fond of movements.

Climbing the cracked slate steps, she rapped noisily on the elaborately paneled, termite-damaged main door. Petro's hearing wasn't what it had once been. Wyn, impatient, opened the door and called her name.

Her voice echoed a bit around the rotunda foyer but there was no answer. Perhaps Petro's in the loo, Wyn thought, and then realized the water hookup was probably disconnected. Not that that would stop Petro.

Wyn called out again. The room with its plaster friezes and dome roof was creepy. Authentically creepy. And heavy with the stench of mildew.

There was no response, so Wyn walked in. The shadows on the cracked plaster walls and the background sound of the ocean in mild turmoil didn't comfort her. She didn't much like un-lived-in places.

This one, reeking of major damp and minor animal deposits, felt especially desolate. Wyn had progressed a few feet into the circular foyer when she recognized Petronella's going-to-court shoes: orange and low heeled, their toes pointed heavenward. The rest of her was half hidden by the marble central staircase.

Suspecting seizure or stroke, Wyn walked quickly to the spot where Petronella lay. It took her a minute to figure out what the hell that thing was twisted around Petro's neck, but she finally saw it was a pair of blue panty hose.

Petro's face was a much paler blue than the panty hose, which had been tightly wrapped. She wore a parody of the smile she had employed for most of her adult life in greeting potential clients. It indicated the sort of social poise that came hand in white glove with superior breeding. This last, thin-lipped rictus made Wyn, now on her knees searching for a pulse that wasn't beating, unexpectedly miserable.

With distaste and trepidation and a sour taste in her mouth, she moved away, guiltily reassuring herself that there was no call to employ the kiss of life, that Petronella St. Cloud was beyond her help.

She left the house and used her cellular telephone to notify the authorities as she wiped away the unanticipated wetness around her eyes. Petronella St. Cloud had been relentlessly mean and self-serving but she had been her own woman, always, and hadn't deserved this joke ending.

Later, Shadows came alive for one last moment. The techies arrived with their lights and noise. They crawled around, armed with plastic bags and tweezers and tiny, high-powered flashlights.

Wyn stood outside, leaning against Petro's car, feeling suspended in time and gratefully numb. This protective balloon was popped by a doofus of a detective named Pasko, who pointed out that the killer might still have been in the house when Wyn was bent over the unrevivable Petronella.

It's too late for hysterics, Wyn told herself, but that

didn't stop her from having her own version of them, which entailed a rigid countenance and a tight-mouthed cellular call home. Tommy arrived fifteen minutes later, his mother driving.

It took a quarter of an hour of animated conversation with Pasko, and another cellular call to the Waggs Neck Harbor chief of police, Homer Price, before Wyn could extricate herself.

Tommy sent his mother and her Honda on their way. Driving the Jaguar with one hand, his free arm around Wyn, he muttered there-there's. He knew Wyn wouldn't thank him for taking her right to the hospital emergency room, but he had never seen her anywhere near this spaced out.

As they approached the West Sea Hospital emergency entrance, Wyn sat up and told him she was fine.

"Yeah, right," Tommy said, unconvinced.

"I'm fine enough not to have to submit to the ER butcher brigade's pinchings and probings." This convinced Tommy that she probably was. "Who the hell," she wanted to know, looking at herself in the visor mirror, not liking what she saw, "would want to murder Petro?"

"Get real, Wyn," Tommy said, heading for home. "The line would stretch from here to Secaucus and back."

Once safe inside the house she had grown up in, Wyn kicked off the offending red shoes and found Probity waiting for her, tail awag. The two of them lay down on the green sofa, holding one another close, inhaling each other's distinctive scents.

After a moment, Tommy joined them, wrapping his muscular arms around Wyn, which is what she wanted in the first place. Only then did she close her remarkable eyes and allow a picture to develop: Petro—turbaned head, clanking pearls, and hooded lids—came to light like a slow-developing Polaroid.

Despite the comforting embrace of dog and man, Wyn cried. She didn't cry easily but when she did, her tears were copious and painful.

Wyn ordered herself to stop with the tears, but she couldn't. She found she had genuinely cared for the old harridan and mourned her loss. "Who the hell," she asked again, "would've wanted to kill Petro?"

Chapter

3

⤸

"THIS COULD BE THE BIG KAHUNA," PASKO SAID TO HIMSELF with uncharacteristic optimism.

He was daydreaming, basking in the continuing spring sunshine, sitting on the plastic bench facing the disconsolate West Sea Judicial Complex parking lot, a quarter filled with nondescript cars.

It was nine A.M. on the Monday following the Saturday when Petronella's body had been found. He had spent Sunday morning at the gym, his mind going a mile a minute as he bench-pressed his weight: one hundred and sixty-two honed and toned pounds.

By Sunday afternoon he was at the keyboard of the shared computer terminal in the outer office, dredging up information on past cases. His lack of facility with the computer was frustrating; he wanted to stop cocking around with bullshit codes. He wanted to reach inside the damn thing and pull out what he needed with his fists.

On Sunday night, exhausted but hopeful, he had gone to bed in the narrow bare-bones West Sea townhouse he rented. He was pretty certain, please Jesus, that this case was the opportunity for which he had been waiting nearly a decade.

Thus he was anxious to get started on this bright Monday morning but there were, as always, obligations to be met. The first was Cora. She had given him an ultimatum: a private meeting or a public scene. She had accepted, after wrangling, this semiprivate meeting place. She wanted satisfaction.

The West Sea Judicial Complex had been built thanks to a perceived rise in crime in this east end of Suffolk County. Insiders knew the crime rate numbers had been inflated but no one much objected to a severe, unnecessary ten-million-dollar building bringing jobs and bribes to the constituency.

In addition to Pasko's and Cora's offices, it contained six courtrooms, a forensic crime laboratory, and enough electronic equipment to run the next world war.

"These pussies," Pasko said in his weekly call to his adviser, a captain in Manhattan's Sixth Precinct who served as Pasko's "rabbi." "Like they call this a hotbed of crime. It's as hot as Siberia."

"If you keep your nose clean . . ." the captain began.

"Like it wasn't my nose that got me into trouble in the first place."

"This is true," the captain agreed, amused; he loved Pasko as if he were a bad son. "You keep that clean, too. What you need, Pasko, is a big win out there. Then we maybe can bring you back."

He'd been saying that for nearly ten years, ever since Pasko had been fired from the NYPD Detective Division for conduct unbecoming. It was a stale scenario: One of the money men behind the current mayor had arrived home unexpectedly to find Pasko in his bed and in his wife.

Later, Pasko's captain, that Catholic rabbi, had arranged a job out here at the end of nowhere. To get back to the action, as the rabbi often told him, Pasko needed a triumph.

His father and his two uncles and several cousins had all been cops in the Hell's Kitchen section of Manhattan, not one of them ever rising to anything like prominence, mostly because they didn't care for prominence.

Pasko and his mother did, and he had gotten himself a good start in Manhattan, making lieutenant detective by the time he was twenty-six, mostly on the strength of the fact that he was relentless, had a few breaks in difficult cases, and possessed a laconic style that was popular with the men. And the women.

"He's not all that tall but like he is so buff. Like he's got this wrestler's body and big bruiser hands and buns of molten steel. And like he talks like this." Cora, Pasko's most recent conquest, lowered her voice several octaves, put chin to magnificent chest, and said, " 'Yo, how's it hangin', guy?' "

Cora, *the* computer jockey in the West Sea crime research department, was an important conduit to and from the FBI's criminal files and the National Crime Network. She was the department's source of genuine information, a woman of thirty often described as "one hot little redhead."

Pasko knew he might be doing himself in by dumping Cora. But, he rationalized, making one of his usual mistakes, there were other computer jockeys and he already had his eye on a sweet brunette who had legs that wouldn't stop.

Cora had brought about her own ruin by foolishly confiding in one of the secretaries who came and went with regularity. "That pouty lower lip. Like he's permanently pissed off. I just want to bite it. And that gangsta way of walking. You know, I could marry that bastard tomorrow. Don't think I'm not working on it." She gave a tiny fake laugh, trying out the idea: "Like maybe I'll get knocked up by accident. It worked for my old lady."

When Pasko had this conversation repeated to him by any number of co-workers—Cora's voice tended to carry—he went into complete dissociation. No phone calls. No drop-ins at the computer department. He thought it was the quick and painless way. And it was. For him.

Cora, who knew why, stormed out of the ground-floor glass doors demanding to know why. She was wearing a flattering peach-colored wrap-around dress, virginal makeup, and Kitty Kelly three-inch-heel sandals that made her nearly as tall as he.

Not getting up from the bench, Pasko explained slowly, carefully, in his deadpan way that "for me, Cora, marriage is like death. Fucking the same person for forty years . . . that's like nuts. And who'd want to? Kids? People got to be crazy to have kids. I was born a free man. I'm going to remain one."

"What about love?" Cora wanted know, grasping either elbow, her cute snub nose pointing up at him accusingly. "What about love?" she asked, as if playing a trump card.

Pasko said he didn't know nothing about love and didn't much want to. He stood up and got into his sporty gray V8 Cougar with the moon roof.

"Where you going?" Cora wanted to know, real tears

in her eyes, smudgeless mascara smudging. "I'm not through."

"Yeah you are."

I'm going, he answered silently, to save my so-called career and my so-called life by finding out who strangled Petronella St. Cloud. Lord Jesus and half the male population of West Sea knew that Cora could take care of herself.

Chapter

4

Neither Wyn nor Tommy had done laundry over the weekend. Petronella's demise had put paid to any useful household occupation. As a result, Wyn was not wearing undergarments on this drear Tuesday morning and regretting it.

A sharp breeze coming from the bay was finding its way up her skirt to what her mother called "the nether regions." Wyn was going to have to buy a pair of something—not panty hose—as soon as this funeral was over.

The funeral wasn't Petronella's. Petro's body had not yet been released to her proper down-island heirs, who, given the sensational way in which she died, planned a tasteful, ultraprivate crematorium good-bye.

Wyn distrusted the rituals of death and had vowed any number of times never to attend another funeral; but good intentions gave way before societal pressure and she felt that if she didn't attend Myra Fiske Stein's sendoff, she'd let herself in for a goodly amount of village opprobrium.

Besides, Myra had been A-okay in Wyn's book even though she had been monumentally misguided about her business acumen. Rosy-cheeked and wide of girth, Myra should have been a mother of seven—her pecan pies were delicious and her darning superb—but instead, after her husband died when their only issue was ten, she had turned her full attention not to regeneration but to the waning Fiske family fortunes.

That only son, Wyn's longtime friend LeRoy, had suffered and not merely from the lack of his mother's interest. He had inherited her foolishness when it came to investments.

Wyn, who had relied on Myra for her devil-may-care optimism and gravy-laden Sunday chicken dinners, had felt true affection for her.

But she didn't want to dwell on Myra's death; it had been too long in coming. The upside of local funerals, Wyn reflected, attempting a Myra-like positive spin on the ultimate negative situation, was the old cemetery. Disintegrating headstones and turn-of-the-century mausoleums were watched over by giant oaks that nearly blotted out the spring sky. It was an integral part of village life, and though Wyn avoided sentimentality, sentimental was the way she felt about the cemetery.

Still, that didn't mean she had to pay attention to the self-important minister spouting irritating truisms. Like so many others attendant, Wyn busied herself counting the house. The usuals had turned out for the final goodbye to one of the town's Brahmins. Women of a certain age all dolled up in weathered hats and faded black dresses with accordion-pleated skirts from another, more formal era. Their black Red Cross shoes may have looked like standard Third Reich army issue, but Wyn forgave them: Elderly feet demanded substance.

A few thin gentlemen in dark suits and white shirts provided gender balance, a number of them supported by aluminum canes. The Old Guard. After all, Myra had been a descendant of one of the earliest village families even if she had married a foreigner. She was due their respect. Besides, as one deaf codger shouted to another, nothing enlivens a Tuesday morning like a funeral.

Wyn leaned against the front door of her own family's mausoleum—a brownstone Greek temple, circa 1886—trying not to tune in to the static of the minister. Feeling Tommy's strong arm through the thick corduroy of his sports jacket, Wyn looked up at him and told herself that she was lucky. If her first husband had been an exquisite Middle Eastern ceramic tile, Tommy was a solid American brick.

Tommy, that sincere person, was taking at face value every pretentious thought that came popping out of the minister's mouth. It would seem as if the man had never known the deceased instead of seeing her in church every Sunday for the past half century. For one insane moment Wyn was tempted to step forward, shut the old boy up, and talk about the real Myra Fiske Stein: She had been good and kind and, despite her unfortunate way with investments, a genuine model for the women of the village.

Tommy, sensing something uncool in the air, grabbed his wife's soft hand in his rough one, draining her of outrage, instilling common sense.

Certainly, Wyn reflected, the chief mourner, LeRoy Stein, would not be amused by her taking over the pulpit. She looked with an exasperated affection at what was presumably the last of the Steins.

LeRoy Stein was fortyish and oversized in a Humpty-Dumpty fashion. A firm believer in clothes making the man, today he was turned out like a Middle European baron on a grouse hunt. He stood on wide, flat feet encased in argyle socks and handmade brogues, intent on every word the minister was mouthing, as if he were receiving a benediction.

Wyn was aware that under his facade LeRoy was deeply upset. His mother, who had believed wrongly that LeRoy could look after himself, had been the sole object of his affection for most of his life. After she suffered a debilitating stroke and had to be warehoused at the understaffed Bide-a-Wee nursing home, a small, important chunk of LeRoy's ego seemed to crumble and disappear.

Wyn had known LeRoy since both were little and their mothers had put them together for the express purpose of "learning the socializing process." Later, they'd escort one another down to the long-gone Main Street Sweet Shoppe, where Wyn would choose strawberry laces and elegant LeRoy would pick marzipan fruit.

Wyn's mother hadn't really encouraged the friendship between the two children. "He's the kind of boy who grows up to take little girls into vacant lots," she had predicted. For once, she hadn't been prescient.

LeRoy had become not a sexual monster but instead, stepping into his mother's boots, a self-pronounced (and failed) "environmentally sound" developer. Carried away by the vision of a new, green America, LeRoy's dreams had centered not on ravishing little girls but on transforming the old, defunct village watch factory into environmentally correct housing.

For a time, the Watch Factory Condos had looked as if they might succeed—this had been five years ago—

and the banks and other investors had supplied LeRoy with much too much capital. He had gone on to purchase acreage off Swamp Road in the mistaken belief that it might be developed ("No way," said the environmental tsars) and then had to sell that at a considerable loss. Meanwhile, lack of interest in living in the old watch factory had brought that project to a screaming, bankrupt halt.

Leaving his comatose mother in the Bide-a-Wee, LeRoy had next gone west to the bombed-out Bronx, joining a movement composed of the rich playing poor, all attempting to revive the sadly diminished Grand Concourse.

Failure followed him like a defective gene as evidenced by his sure hand in choosing doomed projects. Bankrolled by an unnamed sponsor, LeRoy left the Bronx and moved on to central Florida, where Wyn had hoped he would have a better chance—though the idea of a swamp-bordered condominiumized trailer park miles from any swimmable/fishable water hadn't sounded promising.

Alerted by the Bide-a-Wee staff that his mother was in extremis, LeRoy had recently returned home to the Water Street cottage to which the Steins had been reduced in later years.

"Florida was a grand critical success," LeRoy lied, during a homecoming dinner with Wyn and Tommy. His distress over his mother's condition was temporarily soothed by the free-range chicken and tofu casserole Tommy had cooked. "I'll be rolling in it in a few years when the last of the trailers have been paid off. Then I'll take Mother to the best doctors, I'll . . ."

"LeRoy," Wyn said, passing him Tommy's homemade potato bread, "your mother is dying." It took gumption to say this so baldly, but nuance where

LeRoy was concerned was nearly always a waste of energy.

"What do those Bide-a-Wees know about anything?" he said dismissively. His next plan, he confided, was to construct ecologically sound waterfront housing off western Bay Street. He alerted Tommy, a master carpenter, that he would be relying on him. "Don't take on any long-range projects. Soon as I get the capitalization together, it's a go, trust me."

"LeRoy," Wyn said, "you may be the last reasonably educated person in America who believes the green movement has commercial possibilities."

"I do," LeRoy said as if he were taking marriage vows, scraping his plate clean. "Tommy, is there any more of that homemade applesauce?" Tommy, proud of his New Age cooking achievements, decanted another sealed mason jar.

After dinner, the three of them sat on the front porch reminiscing, LeRoy delicately blowing his own horn into the blue-black evening, though he did finally admit that the banks had nixed his new project.

"But I'm courting Lettitia Browne," he whispered in a small confidence, revealing old news. He had agreed to be the unpaid working chair of the New Federal Inn's centenary celebration in the hope that owner Lettie would bankroll the shoreline condominiums he had in mind.

Later, as Tommy held Wyn in his sculpted arms, he asked, "You think Lettie's going to put money into a new LeRoy Stein project?"

"Please," Wyn said, snuggling closer. "Lettie needed someone like LeRoy—pretentious, goal-driven, unsalaried, blind to reality—to put together the New Federal's centennial celebration. LeRoy," she said, switching position, having Tommy hold her from behind, "is perfect.

His mother's family founded the hotel back in the 1800s and he'll do almost anything for money as long as it has a prestigious ring to it."

One of Tommy's big, calloused hands moved down her body while the other moved up. "I only hope that after the centenary Lettie will offer him a paying job," Wyn said, pretending to ignore those roving digits, squirming a bit anyway. "The collars of his custom shirt looked a bit despondent, don't you think?"

"Didn't notice," Tommy said, intent on what he was about.

"What are you doing, Handwerk?" Wyn asked, as if she didn't know, a virgin in a seducer's hands.

"What do you think I'm doing, Lewis?"

This funeral had really gone on much too long, Wyn decided, sorry to glimpse tears flowing freely down Le-Roy's cheeks. His tears reminded her of how much he had wanted his mother's undivided love and how ignorant of that fact Myra had been.

Poor Myra and her dumb marriage. LeRoy's father, Roman, had been a sloe-eyed, ascot-adorned postwar European emigré who had descended on the village in 1945 and swept orphaned Myra off her village princess's feet via a lightning seduction.

The village was aghast but Myra, a naïf to the end, wore a "be happy" smile on her plain face, wore it up to the very end, which occurred when her husband died of pneumonia on LeRoy's tenth birthday in September of 1965.

Instead of retiring quietly into the Fiske cottage and looking about for a new, more suitable second husband, Myra decided to become a business person.

She took control of her inherited real estate holdings, which included the watch factory and the family's hotel, the New Federal Inn. Husband Stein had not been much of a business manager but he had managed to keep the Fiske property intact. Myra had always felt he was old-fashioned and now there was no stopping the new, liberated Myra and her advanced business ideas.

It took her twenty-odd years to lose everything.

Early on, she made a down payment on that troubled Southampton oceanfront estate, Shadows, and moved herself and LeRoy in. The selling broker, Petronella St. Cloud, gave Myra a private mortgage for the amount owed at a rate considered extortionist by most.

By the mid-1980s, all of Myra's properties needed serious upgrading. Rather than improving what she had, Myra made the classic mistake of untried, desperate developers. By now she had some idea of where she stood and decided to risk it all on one big gamble. She hocked herself up to her pretty green eyeballs and— together with another naïf, a junkyard dealer named Flinty Jones—bought the duck farm property from the Bells.

The land had been liberated from town constraints by the zoning board and Myra and Flinty planned a grand hotel in the European luxe tradition.

It was only after she and Flinty closed on the duck farm that Myra learned there wasn't a bank in the world that would lend her money on such a project. Deluxe hotels were not what Southampton tourists wanted; and in any case, neither Myra nor Flinty had experience in hotel construction, much less management. When Myra reminded the various loan committees of her New Federal Inn experience, that became another nail in her fiscal coffin: The New Federal hadn't shown a profit since she had taken over its management.

On the day her properties were sold at auction on

the county courthouse steps, Myra Fiske Stein, finally realizing she had lost all of her family's assets, experienced the stroke that condemned her to spend her last ten years comatose in the Bide-a-Wee nursing home.

LeRoy had vowed to restore the family fortunes, but as far as Wyn could tell, nothing had been restored despite LeRoy's recent tale of the successful Florida trailer park condominiumization and his plans for Bay Street housing.

As Myra Fiske Stein was finally lowered into the sandy soil of the Waggs Neck Harbor cemetery (her family had held mausoleums to be pretentious), Wyn kissed LeRoy's damp cheek and Tommy hugged him in the new manly fashion. Wyn reflected that LeRoy had only wanted what most of us do: his mother's love. Now he didn't have a shot.

"Oh, no," Wyn said to herself as they turned to leave.

Detective Pasko, sitting nonchalantly on the cemetery wall, gave her a small nod of recognition and Wyn felt a tiny jolt of something like guilt.

Tommy sped off, late for a kitchen installation in an East Hampton seaside Palladian hunting lodge. Wyn walked slowly toward Pasko, finally identifying the source of that shard of guilt sticking in her gullet.

It seemed not possible but in the wake of Myra's Sunday morning death, she had forgotten all about Petronella St. Cloud's Saturday morning departure. Tuesday's child, Pasko, the chipper New York sewer rat, was here to remind her.

Chapter

5

PASKO HAD SPEED-READ THE MEDICAL EXAMINER'S REPORT ON Petronella's death ("mechanical asphyxiation"; no shit, Dick Tracy) as he smoked up West Sea Road in his Cougar, destination: Waggs Neck Harbor.

He wasn't all that knowledgeable about Waggs Neck, having been there only once, at night, to have a drink at the New Federal Inn, which Cora considered truly fancy. Pasko thought it "another rinky-dink dump" and they had argued about it. She had cried. Her tears-to-order always tickled him.

Seeing Waggs Neck on a cool spring day, he was equally tickled by the narrow streets lined by authentic gingerbreaded cottages and the double-wide Main Street featuring ye olde brick shops built in maybe 1960. It was a fairy tale village, nothing real about it. Cora, he knew, would give her two-carat diamanté earrings to live there.

He had a ten-second fantasy in which he and Cora

were living in a picket fence-surrounded village cottage, rose-covered wallpaper in the bathroom, dishes adorned with daisies in the dinette. I'd rather die young, he told himself, not realizing it was too late for that.

He hated one-horse towns where, as he told Cora, the busybodies kept a count on how many times a day you farted. He loved New York. There you could live next to someone for fifty years and still not know his name. Get a life, dude, he told himself, hating the fact that ten years later he was still homesick for the Big Apple. Trouble was, he wanted his old life.

He parked the Cougar in the village parking lot, taking up two spaces so some local bozo wouldn't scratch his Simonized finish. With his choreographed give-my-regards-to-Broadway strut, Pasko looked and felt as out of place on Main Street as a Chevy in a Cadillac showroom. Mickey Spillane in St. Mary Meade.

He took satisfaction in this as Tuesday afternoon plastic-curlered heads turned and said, My my in his wake. There wasn't an overabundance of attractive, youngish men in the village exuding carnal knowledge, instant availability, and potential danger.

At Waggs Neck Harbor Realty he was informed by Liz Lum, Wyn Lewis's "executive assistant" and life-long friend that Wyn could be found at the Waggs Neck Harbor cemetery.

"No one's whacked her, have they?"

Liz simpered, though she had long been aware that simpering was not attractive in a nearly six-foot-tall female. Then, returning to her more comfortable cut-and-dried delivery, Liz said, "No, Wyn is very much alive."

She escorted him to the village map that covered most of one office wall and pointed out the cemetery's location. As Liz watched him head off in the appropriate direction, she felt a bit melancholy. Detective Pasko was the hottest hunk she had met in a long time and she knew her chances of getting anywhere with him, let alone to home base, were slim.

Pasko had no trouble spotting Wynsome Lewis among the mourners at the older end of the cemetery. Her husband's undisciplined corn-blond locks and her own sculpted white-blond hair acted as a pair of high-powered beacons lighting the way. All the other colors attendant upon this ceremony were grim and discouraging.

Pasko itched to jump right in, grab the good-looking— all right, great-looking—Wyn Lewis, sit her down, and find out what the hell she knew, if anything.

In New York that might have played. Not here. After a decade in the East End, he was hip enough to know that he had to wait at least until the coffin was in the ground before he made his move. He passed the time, sitting on the cemetery's rough stone wall, which did nothing for his butt, going over his mental notes.

Since Petronella St. Cloud's body had been found with the panty hose wrapped around her neck, every man, woman, and bisexual loosely connected with local law enforcement for the past decade thought it important to remind him of the two lady lawyers who were iced in the same way ten years ago. Like he really needed reminding.

Pasko had been the detective in charge of those murders, which had been committed with the same modus operandi used on Petronella St. Cloud. That case had supposedly been his ticket to ride. He was going to solve it with his usual speedy panache and then return to Manhattan and decide which precinct's offer he would accept.

Except that by the time he came along, everyone was

hip to the fact that the case was unsolvable. And had he used what passed for his brain, Pasko would have realized it too, because if it had been an easy solve, his cock-sucking boss, the evil Captain Savage, would have taken it himself.

And it wasn't like a little case that everyone would forget. Those murders, which would barely have been commented on in Manhattan, caused pandemonium in the East End. Two young professional women, local in the bargain, strangled with panty hose on succeeding peaceful Saturday spring mornings in what should have been the sanctity of their offices in downtown Southampton . . .

Pasko not only did not get back to Manhattan, he started his new Long Island career with the nasty odor of failure following him like a dog with the runs. It had taken him two years of successful solves to dilute it and even today—well especially today—he'd catch an occasional whiff from the past.

Like why else would Captain Savage so readily hand him the Petronella St. Cloud whacking? A wiser, older Pasko knew that it was because Savage believed it unsolvable; that the media, starved for gristle, was bringing up the old cases, marrying them to the new, not sparing Pasko, a favorite target; that it looked as if Pasko had as much a chance of finding the perp as he did of coming upon eternal enlightenment.

Pasko was going to give it a try, mostly out of desperation. If he couldn't be a detective in Manhattan, then all right, he'd be a detective out in the boonies. But if he couldn't be that, he didn't want to be anything. What scared him was that Savage was waiting for a big goof on Pasko's part to get rid of him, and this new murder, coupled with the old, fit the bill.

So there he was, sitting in Waggs Neck Harbor's cemetery, trying to decide if anybody other than a random maniac would want to kill Penny McFee and Harriet Leverage, and then wait ten years before icing Petronella St. Cloud.

What *was* the connection, if any, between McFee, Leverage, and St. Cloud? Female professionals? Eastern Long Island natives and residents? All white? Two WASPs. One Jew. Had the ladies all worked on a lawsuit—one concerning real estate and legalities and money—that some cuckoo bird believed unfair enough to merit strangulation?

But why wait ten long ones to get even with Petronella?

With a chilly feeling in his gut, Pasko realized that if he wanted to get the answers to those questions in a timely fashion, he was going to have to eat humble pie, sooner rather than later. He was going to have to beg Cora to do her magic with computers to track down and cross-check the three victims' associations. He had already approached the black-haired computer chick with the legs that wouldn't stop, but she told him, huffily, that all requests for information had to go through Cora. Loyal bitch.

One question he didn't have to ask himself was if he was going to have to pledge undying love and marriage and fuck Cora four ways to Sunday to get her to cooperate. He knew the answer.

Haunting him was the possibility that there was no connection between those early victims, McFee and Leverage. And no connection between their murders and Petronella's. That random nut cases were the killers, copying off one another. This was the theory to which Captain A-hole Savage subscribed, and not just because he did, Pasko felt it was wrong.

Or hoped it was wrong. He couldn't escape the feeling that he was spinning wheels, digging himself deeper into the West Sea slime, burying himself forever.

Because if the killer *was* a random nutsky, Pasko knew he had as much chance of finding him as he had of making commissioner. Random nut cases required an army of police and a battery of computers, not to mention endless time and Jobian patience, none of which Pasko possessed.

The bottom line was that he had to disregard the random maniac theory; if he was wrong and random proved valid, he was going to have trouble keeping himself from jumping off Shark Channel Bridge.

In the meantime he was going to interview Miss Butter-Wouldn't-Melt, find out if she knew anything and what she was doing later when her old man wasn't around.

Chapter

6

~~~

PASKO SUGGESTED GOING BACK TO WYN'S OFFICE.

"To catch up on old times?" Wyn asked, communicating her dislike of that idea.

"To see if I can dig out of you what you know about Petronella St. Cloud's murder, seeing as you were the person who found her."

Though the local daily bugles were using ten-inch type to rake up the old McFee-Leverage murders, though a brain like Wyn's had to have made the McFee-Leverage-St. Cloud connection, Pasko himself was keeping off the topic, waiting to see if she'd mention it. "What about the coffee shop?" he asked. "Think you'll be safe enough there?"

She hadn't felt threatened, but she didn't want half the village witnessing her being grilled in her office window and the other half hearing it via the village hotline moments later.

A bit chastened, she led the way to the semiprivate

back banquette in the Eden Café. "This is where the mayoress and her clique like to lunch," she said brightly, wondering why on earth she had assumed this very strange role: slightly dizzy postdeb.

"Awesome," Pasko said, taking the seat facing the back door, confused. The other day she had seemed a little bitchy but a regular sort of highfalutin woman . . . if anyone who looked and presented herself like she did could be called regular. Today she was about as natural as Burt Reynolds's hairpiece.

Wyn was aware, and not merely from her odd language patterns, that she was feeling, as her dad once said, nervy. She was receiving strange vibrations from inner space. Anxiety was lurking somewhere around her midriff, shaking her tummy up, and though she denied it, she thought she knew why.

She honestly did not think she was being paranoid when the thought occurred to her while she was walking Probity that morning that there was a possibility of mayhem in her future.

"If some loon strangled Petro," she asked Probity, busy doing her business on a much-abused bit of village park, "because she was a successful lady Realtor, what's to keep that same loon from murdering *moi?*"

The media was filled with cases of specialized coconuts who attacked bleached blondes, one-armed prostitutes, choirboys between the ages of eleven and twelve. She was aware that for her day-to-day sanity, she was going to have to put this idea back in the bottomless well of her mind; once dredged up, however, that wasn't so easy.

Currently making her less than comfortable was Pasko with his mean street sensuality and that famished way he looked at her. His lonely blue-tinged air of total self-reliance reminded her of someone, and when what passed for coffee finally arrived, she was afraid she knew who. Herself.

Intimacy, real or imagined, jarred her and it was only Tommy's velvet-gloved insistence that had made her give in to both his and her needs to know someone; to know one another. Still, in moments of high trepidation—when miasmic foreboding filled the air—she preferred to be curled up in the classic fetal position on the green sofa, wrapped up in her father's old Indian blanket, sublimely isolated.

Wyn decided to get a grip, to be herself (whoever that was) while Pasko read the oversized plastic menu as if he were committing it to memory. Satisfied that he had explored all his Eden Café options, he asked, "What are you so scared about?" When Wyn didn't answer—she was hardly about to bare her soul to Pasko—he threw a well-worn ringer into the game. "You see yourself as the principal suspect?"

"No," Wyn said.

"You always this bubbly?" She looked really scared. He wanted to put his mitt on her hand and say sorry. That, of course, was not the way official investigations were conducted and she didn't look like she'd welcome his hand anyway.

"I didn't know this was a social occasion," Wyn returned. "Look, do you think we can get on with it?" Now she felt she had changed roles, more Lauren Bacall than Carole Lombard.

"What can I get you?" Mary Jane Eden, Thelma Eden's preternaturally ripe daughter, pad in hand, green gum in mouth, Wonderbra in place, wanted to know, easily breaking the mood.

"Whatcha got?" Pasko asked, cocking his head, laying on the toughness.

"She's got a really nice fiancé who happens to be a

40

village policeman. Taller and younger than you," Wyn said.

"Good with his dukes?" Pasko asked with mock seriousness.

"You wouldn't last half a round. However, if you and Mary Jane care to continue this mating dance, I'll excuse myself and return to work."

Pasko said he'd have a cup of coffee and a BLT. Wyn ordered a slice of the Eden's weighty pound cake and a diet Coke, light on the ice. Mary Jane, batting Maybelline's finest eyelashes, moved on.

"How do you detect?" Wyn asked, as if she were interested. She was again changing moods, trying to be sympathetic in the man-had-a-job-to-do vein. There was no reason for her to be so mean-tempered even though Pasko was a sexist slug. And of course she did want Petro's murderer apprehended. As for her own worries, maybe she should go on Prozac as her social worker ex-sister-in-law had so often suggested.

There was always a war going on in her: her dad elevating everyone to princelike status, her mother treating everyone like a garden pest. Middle ground was what Wyn tried for, but it so often eluded her.

She felt so taut at this point, she only wanted to relax. Not that the Eden regulars, elderly pensioners, at the front counter were helping her become less self-conscious. They had spun around on their revolving counter stools so they could face Wyn while they continued to slurp their beverages. Better than the television, it was commonly agreed.

"I use the process of elimination," Pasko told Wyn, eyeing Mary Jane as she served the burnt BLT. He was thinking she was hot and available but he didn't need to alienate the countess sitting across the table from him or the local constabulary. Mary Jane would keep.

"I get all the suspects lined up and, one by one, using interviews and background checks, I eliminate them until only the perp is left."

"Who have you eliminated so far in Petronella's murder?" Wyn asked politely.

"The down-island periodontist nephew who inherited big time. He was coaching his son's Little League team all Saturday morning and there's half a dozen pissed-off mothers who attest to the fact. Like the worm favors his own kid. Guy might have hired someone to do auntie . . . but if he wanted her money, he would have had her iced a few years ago when he was in school and needed it."

"Who else?" Wyn asked.

"You," Pasko said, giving her a hint of his never-fail killer smile.

"Me?" Wyn asked, again surprised at this suggestion.

"Like you were there, right? Like you wouldn't be the first killer in history to pretend to find the victim."

"And why would I kill Petronella?"

"That remains to be seen, as Sherlock Holmes used to say."

"I don't think Sherlock Holmes ever said that and I don't think you seriously suspect me." She dusted her hands free of stale pound cake crumbs, attempting to let him know that she was dusting his suspicion off as well.

He placed his mini–tape recorder on the table in front of her. "You want to run through it again?"

"No, I do not want to run through it again."

"Here or in West Sea?"

"Didn't I sign a paper attesting to the fact that . . ."

"Let's go."

Wyn knew he meant it and so she ran through it

again from the time she made the appointment with Petro to the moment she called the police.

"What'd you leave out?" he asked, after she was finished.

"*Rien*, which means 'nothing' in French."

"You may not know this but I got a thing for broads who treat me like horse manure." He flipped off the tape recorder, satisfied. This account agreed substantially with Wyn's earlier one.

"You must have your hands full," Wyn couldn't resist saying.

"Listen, you ever fool around?"

"I don't have the time. In fact . . ." Wyn started to get up.

"All right. Park it for a minute."

" 'Broads.' 'Park it for minute.' You get all your dialogue from Frank Sinatra?"

"My favorite uncle did twenty hard ones in the can."

"That explains a great deal," Wyn said, resuming her seat and taking up her mother's high school principal voice.

"You should've been a teacher," Pasko said, getting it in one.

"Listen, Detective Pasko, if we can't keep this conversation on a nonpersonal level . . ."

"Chill. Close your eyes. Relax your body. Describe to me exactly what you saw when you walked around the staircase and found Petronella St. Cloud."

Wyn made a noise that sounded like "tchah" but did as Pasko asked. He had switched the recorder back on. "At first I thought Petro had had a stroke. Her torso was in the shadow cast by the staircase but I recognized her shoes. Everything was so neat, so nicely arranged. Unlike Petro, whose personal style was high messy.

"Her purse was next to her as if she had placed it

there while she took a nap and she was eccentric enough to do just that. I only realized that something was radically wrong when I bent down and found that was not a scarf around her neck, that it was a pair of panty hose."

"What did you think then?"

Wyn opened her remarkable silver eyes. "I didn't think a darn thing then, Detective. My mind was beyond logic. From that moment on and for most of the day, I did everything by rote. Protective shock."

He decided it was time. "You ever hear of a couple of young ladies by the names of Penny McFee and Harriet Leverage?"

"Yes," Wyn said. "Who in the East End hasn't? They were strangled like Petro, and for a long time after, no woman I knew sat alone in her office on a Saturday morning."

"McFee specialized in real estate law. You ever work with her? Or with Leverage?"

"I worked with them both. Harriet Leverage was a low-level prosecutor for the county, doing a lot of small-potato environmental policing, making a pain in the neck of herself. Lots of enemies. Penny McFee was in private practice. She was a townie—so was Harriet for that matter—pretty and popular and really smart. They were both ambitious. Harriet seemed a touch cutthroat and Penny looked as if she had a permanent-pressed smile on her face. But your Eastern Long Island hip agreed that they were to be watched and probably supported."

Wyn signaled the loitering Mary Jane that she would have another slice of pound cake. Anxiety made her hungry. The cake was served with more coffee and a swollen-eyed glance for Pasko. He seemed to have lost interest.

He wanted to know what direct contacts Wyn had had with the two young women, and Wyn cooperated. Talking about history and real estate made her comfortable. "Penny was the attorney for a number of real estate transactions I worked on. Nineteen eighty-six, right? Only a year after I returned.

"Real estate had died a quick death in Southampton but Waggs Neck had been written up in both *New York* and *The New Yorker* as *the* place to be, so all those semi-impoverished Wall Streeters gave up their aspirations to Gin Lane and convinced themselves falling-down Waggs Neck cottages were the perfect weekend houses. They were snapping them up as if we were giving away the last of the Romanov châteaus."

"Why use a Southampton lawyer?"

"At the time Waggs Neck Harbor attorneys were not all that reliable. Kash, Fellon and Weeps could all be bought for one sorry roast beef sandwich and they were not computerized. Weeps did everything by shaky hand. Penny McFee was reputable and efficient.

"I think Harriet Leverage may have been peripherally involved in the Bell duck farm sale—that was a biggie for me. I was representing both the buyers and the sellers. Penny was the attorney for both parties. This double agent, double attorney method's unusual but money was saved by one and all, and that's what they wanted. I'd have to go back into the files and find out how and if Harriet fit in."

"How about doing me a favor?" Pasko asked, widening his navy blue eyes. "And like work up a detailed account of the duck farm sale and any other deals you might have worked on with the three victims?"

Pasko was working at being especially couth, aware, as he was, of a familiar, pleasant/painful tingling behind the zippered crotch of his trousers. Wynsome

45

Lewis was exactly the kind of woman he always wanted and rarely got. She was a ten-pound box of Godiva chocolates. Most of his conquests were dime Hershey's Kisses.

"No," Wyn said, getting up. "I wouldn't do it for you. But I'll do it for Penny, Harriet, and Petro." While the sentiment was real, this last line sounded so stupid and high-toned, Joan of Arc moral that Wyn blushed.

Pasko, intent on his tape recorder, didn't appear to notice. "Like by tomorrow?"

"Like by the end of the week."

Wyn had stood up and Pasko leaned forward with great sincerity, staring up at her with what he hoped was his dying boy's last-request look. "Any chance we can get it together like real privately before then?"

"Next time you're in the village, Detective, I'd very much like you to meet my husband."

"Yeah?" Pasko asked, grinning. "So he can knock my block off?"

"No. So you can see why you're not now and never will be in the competition."

"Like I wasn't asking for a lifetime commitment," Pasko said.

She left him with the check and Mary Jane and a sour taste in his mouth. Maybe it was the Eden's burnt BLT.

There was a rude sound from his beeper. When he checked in with Savage's hostile secretary and told her where he was, she said, "Wow, that is like karma, dude. Captain wants you to go over and talk to Waggs Neck Chief of Police Homer Price. He's been attached to the case; he's going to be working with you."

"Let me talk to the captain," Pasko said, teeth clenched.

"Pity, Pasko. Captain said if you asked to talk to him,

to tell you he's out and that you're working with Homer Price whether you like it or not. It's part of Senator Piet Kennedy's scheme for having county and village law enforcement work with one another. You being white and Homer Price a spade is the icing on the cake. Everyone's going to be watching, Pasko, to make sure you're nice and cooperative."

She gave a mean, genuinely amused laugh and hung up. Pasko, allowing himself the luxury of self-pity, strode down Main Street to the Municipal Building and the damned chief of police of Waggs Neck fuckin' Harbor. "Like I need this," he said to no one in particular.

Chapter

7

EARLY ON WEDNESDAY MORNING, LIZ LUM AND WYN LEWIS were going over odd bits of business and the rest of the week's appointments in the latter's office, Liz wrapped in a vaguely ethnic garment, Wyn in a white and navy-blue Admiralty-inspired suit. Both outfits came from the rad boutique known as Sizzle and were meant, Liz and Wyn realized too late, for younger women.

Luckily, office rules precluded the discussion of personal adornment unless a request was made to do so. Murder, this morning, was also a verboten topic. Wyn wanted to get back on track.

Liz was ready. "Mrs. Bode," she said, rolling her eyes and sighing, "wants a thirteenth day." She made this announcement with grim, don't-look-at-me satisfaction.

"Stop." Mrs. Bode, who billed herself as a smart cookie, had been dithering about selling her dilapidated Bay Street vacation house for months and now that terms and closing dates were finally agreed upon, she had decided she needed an extra day to vacate. The new owner had already rearranged complicated plans in order to move in on the day that had best suited Betty Bode. After the last round of idiotic negotiations, he had declared that if Mrs. Bode made any more unreasonable demands, the deal was kaput.

"Tell Betty," Wyn said, teeth clenched, "that I will personally pay for a hotel in which she may spend the thirteenth day and if that doesn't satisfy her, she can find a new Realtor better equipped to handle her neurosis." The pencil in her grip broke into three pieces.

Ignoring this, Liz went on. "You have an appointment on Saturday with Frank Jones and Merredith Holliday to show them Kathy Carruthers's Montauk listing."

"Good," Wyn said. "I'll make Merrie drive the Rolls-Royce while I recline in the passenger seat, pretending I belong among the privileged. Would you call Kathy and confirm the appointment?"

"Long since done," said the efficient Liz, who privately believed Wyn had always belonged among the privileged.

Wyn had known Frank Jones, seven years her junior and a Waggs Neck Harbor boy, forever. She had only met his sister a decade before when Wyn returned to the village, a nervous new Realtor tentatively finding her way among suspicious townsfolk.

Frank Jones, who had also just returned about that time, had introduced her to Sister Merrie (as he sometimes called her) on a dark winter's day. Wyn, like a good many women and men in the village, was itchy with curiosity about their relationship.

Rumors of Frank's and Merrie's "unnatural" connection had been heating up the village hot line for some time. Wyn subscribed to the belief that "anything goes as long as it affects no one except the parties involved," but she couldn't help but be dismayed by the sulfuric whiff of incest.

Taking a page from her late father's book in dealing with unpleasantness, she elected to ignore what her mother would have called "Biblically proscribed sexual congress" and instead chose the high road, concentrating on the engaging, eccentric personalities of the pair.

Not to mention their histories, which were well known but still endlessly fascinating to those Waggs Neck Harborites who doted on the gossip euphemistically known as "local family background."

Self-styled social Southampton and Waggs Neck Harbor historians could hardly forget Merrie's and Frank's mother, Virginia Holliday. In the staid 1950s, she had been a rebel with a cause, and that had been to make her rich, self-absorbed parents sit up and take notice. It was agreed that Virginia spared them nothing.

Though her efforts weren't effective. The senior Hollidays made all the right moves via bail money and smart attorneys and top-notch psychiatrists but they didn't really seem to care about Virginia.

Nor, for that matter, were they interested in her drab elder sister, Flo, who specialized in Episcopalian good works and never caused her parents a moment's thought.

Virginia, who inherited the Holliday looks but none of the stability, was farmed out during the school year to a small, inflexible Maryland boarding school for girls like her. It was run like a benign penitentiary, situated miles from anywhere that a young girl could get into "mischief."

In summer, however, the Hollidays lived in their

Southampton beachfront mansion, Shadows. At seventeen, Virginia avoided the Bath and Tennis Club set. She managed to locate, in a seedy Waggs Neck bar, the very man she hoped would finally break her parents out of their proper, self-absorbed cocoon.

Flinty Jones was a spare Scots emigré who collected and sold junk for not much of a living in Waggs Neck Harbor village. When Virginia told him that she was pregnant, he said why then he'd marry her. This struck her as exquisitely funny and right and she said sure.

The Hollidays did not run screaming into the streets as the pregnant Virginia had hoped. Instead, they gave her twenty-five thousand dollars and said good-bye forever. Thanks to Petronella St. Cloud, they managed to unload Shadows on Myra Stein and her husband and, with Flo in tow, turned their backs on their unnatural child and fled from Long Island and the United States, settling in London, where Flo became active in the Church of England.

Merredith, Virginia's first child, was so huge she nearly killed her mother in the birth process. The spit image of her aunt Flo, Merrie was, from the beginning, a goal-oriented child.

The marriage between Flinty and Virginia worked out nicely despite everyone's expectations. Somehow, Flinty put out the rage that had been eating away at Virginia's being. She became the sort of person her parents would have wanted her to be, albeit in a different social stratum. She spent a lot of time on her nails and on playing tennis at the public courts as well as performing small-scale charity chores.

The junk business was now in full flower and Flinty began to make money. Merrie was given a bit of a backseat—Virginia had, after all, learned her parenting techniques from her mother—but she was a bossy kid who could and did take care of herself.

When the unplanned baby brother Francis arrived ten years later, Merrie was quick to assume the role of capable little mother. This was just as well because this time Virginia did die after giving birth, and Flinty, who had never quite understood how he had won Virginia, appeared permanently lost.

A number of people wanted to take baby Frank off Merrie's and Flinty's hands. LeRoy Stein's mother, Myra Fiske Stein, bored with widowhood, was in the throes of taking over the family's financial management. But her position as village doyenne demanded that she make the time to take a role in saving the sad Jones household.

Two months after Virginia died, Myra swept down on Jones Junque and announced she had decided to adopt Baby Frank. He would make a nice brother for her son, ten-year-old LeRoy, and she could provide Frank with privileges Flinty never could.

But Flinty had worked his way out of his depression and was proving adept at diapering. Merrie was a great help—so many ten-year-old-girls make excellent mommies—though Flinty hardly noticed. He loved his son with the same tightly focused passion he had reserved for Virginia.

Only slightly daunted, Myra Fiske Stein kept up her interest and found an unlikely friend and fellow cribbage player in the dour Flinty, who was as quiet as she was chatty. They took to spending evenings together while Myra planned Frank's and LeRoy's and Merrie's futures and the fortunes she would make in real estate.

It was an irony much savored locally that Myra was issuing commands, directives, and good advice from Shadows, the house from which Virginia had escaped.

The senior Hollidays had died, leaving Aunt Flo a great deal of money and property in and about London. Hearing of Virginia's death and her new nephew, Flo made a trip home to America with the express idea of taking "Francis off that poor man's hands."

She emerged from her meeting with Flinty with Merrie instead. Merrie railed against this arbitrary separation from her new baby brother but in the end she proved sensible, realizing that at age ten there wasn't much she could do. But patience was her virtue and she was prepared to wait.

She and Aunt Flo lived quietly in London. Merrie—good at sports from the get-go—was considered an asset by the staffs of the British schools she attended. But she was too big and porridgelike and queer in that odd, upper-class American way to be popular with her classmates.

Merrie didn't much care. She already knew that her life was going to be devoted to brother Frank. Over the years she sent him holiday cards and gifts and later, when she came into money of her own, kept up an expensive, important telephone communication. Twice, while visiting New York with Aunt Flo, she managed to see him.

Frank, brought up by his father with Myra Fiske Stein looking over Flinty's shoulder, was a thin beauty of a boy with copper-colored hair and dark, nocturnal eyes. He was a wash at sports but brilliant at theatrics. His fantasy life revolved around his sister swooping down and taking him away from the Jones junkyard, where he and his father lived in what had once been a tin-roofed farmhouse.

Flinty, a man of increasing means but limited capacity, was bewildered by Frank's sharp intelligence and moody temperament. Myra, however, provided intellectual stimulus, affection, and direction. "You get out of the East End as soon as you can," she told Frank. "My husband's mistake was coming here in the first place and staying on in the second. He was a big-time person. So are you, Frank. This is a small-time place."

It only occurred to Frank years later that Flinty and Myra had been sleeping together. Flinty had called her Mrs. Stein; she had responded with Mr. Jones. Neither was the other's first or great love but they had had, in Frank's memory, a great affection for one another and it had only been social restraints that had kept them from marrying. Myra Fiske Stein was the closest the village had to reigning royalty. Flinty was the junkman.

Not surprisingly, Myra's only child, LeRoy, grew up resenting Flinty and, more especially, his son. Frank's charismatic presence at Sunday dinners made LeRoy all the more aware of what he once overheard his mother calling "LeRoy's unfortunate oafishness."

By the early 1980s Flinty had become a rich man. Virginia's twenty-five thousand, invested in enormous amounts of salable junk—rubber, steel, plastic—brought in huge profits. When the time came, Flinty was easily able to put his son through Vassar. Luckily, this was before the real estate bubble that he and Myra Fiske Stein had created burst.

Meanwhile, Merrie had inherited Aunt Flo's estate and was having a jolly time teaching games to British merchants' daughters and escorting Girl Guide expeditions into the English countryside.

But rewarding as this was, Merrie had been marking time, waiting on the sidelines for the right moment to reappear and take her place as coach in the great game of brother Frank's life.

She had understood that Frank had to finish Vassar

without interruption but on graduation day Merrie arrived in Poughkeepsie in her enormous car, and, as in his dreams, whisked Frank away to her newly purchased Fifth Avenue apartment.

They were to live happily ever after, Merrie supporting Frank in some ill-defined artistic endeavor. But Frank's mental balance was not what it might have been; the stresses of engaging in any art proved too much for him, so it was decided that they should return to their Long Island roots.

Merrie loved this idea and thought it would bring comfort and satisfaction to her brother, but she hadn't counted on Francis's moments—days, weeks, months— of withdrawal when even his sister was not allowed entry into his thoughts.

It had been Wyn Lewis who had had to announce to Frank and Merrie that Flinty Jones had been declared a bankrupt, shortly after Myra Stein had her stroke.

"I think you'd better come out and see your dad, Frank," Wyn said. "He's pretty despondent."

Merrie had driven them. They arrived at Jones Junque just before the sun went down. It was Frank who had found Flinty's thin body hanging from a wooden T-bar in his office, perfectly still.

It had been Merrie who had called the police; and Merrie who had asked Wyn to deal with "the legal details"; and Merrie who had pried Frank's arms from their father's legs and arranged for him to spend the rest of the summer in a small, highly regarded Connecticut sanitorium that had, praise the Lord, done the trick.

Frank left the sanitorium in new equestrian style (jodhpurs, boots, riding crop—horseback riding had done wonders for him) with his old love for Merrie intact. But he had new insights into his anger. When

Merrie asked, Frank said he had no other goal than to "make the people of Waggs Neck Harbor eat *merde.*" He blamed them for their father's suicide, for Myra's stroke. He wanted revenge and Merrie, after thinking it over, had to agree that no one had played fair with Flinty or Myra.

The village powers—all members of the business-motivated Main Street Business Society (MSBS)—had long sought to remove Jones Junque from the high-profile corner of Bay Street and Widow Davitt's Road. After Flinty killed himself, they thought they might have a shot. "Revolting thing to see when you take the scenic Bay Street drive, expecting another grand village home and come upon that mess," Mayoress Betty Kunze, the Main Street Business Society's darling, declared on a number of occasions.

But Merrie had been one step ahead of the village board, which dickered too long over buying the property from the bank. She bought it and gave it to Frank, who shut down the junk business but steadfastly refused to remove the merchandise. "Think of it as a monument to Daddy," he whispered loudly into the appalled face of the mayoress, who had come to plead.

Merrie and Frank had moved more or less permanently to the red brick Waggs Neck house once owned by Myra's family. They began by taking advantage of a number of Waggs Neck Harborites, buying rundowns at rock-bottom prices, renovating them on the cheap, and selling them for wonderful profits. True or not, all of the houseowners who had sold to Frank and Merrie claimed they had been swindled. Now, prices doubled whenever Frank and Merrie appeared on a sloping cottage porch that held that illusive potential sidewalk appeal.

Thus the time had come when the village was played out for them and Frank knew it. He felt he had gotten revenge on their father's enemies via the money and the rancor their resales had produced. It was time, he said, to call it a day.

But Merrie had caught the development bug, as she put it. "Why it's the best game ever. And half the time you can make up the rules as you go along." She was already exploring other fields for restoration and profit.

It was assumed by the villagers that Merrie, the boss, would do anything for Frank and she often agreed that this was so. What was less apparent was that Frank would have done anything for Merrie. Which explained his willingness to view properties long after he had lost interest in real estate. "Such a big, sheepdog of a girl," Frank said of her. "She must have been a super gym teacher when she taught those girls in England. Solicitous and kind. Who could help adoring her?"

Dickie ffrench, for one. "Here come the Development Sharks," he said as he watched Merrie adroitly park the Rolls on Lowe Lane on Wednesday morning. He was standing inside his aunt-in-law's house, munching cinnamon toast and sipping Japanese green tea, which had been recommended for his colon. "Don't shut your eyes, Auntie, or they'll steal your underpants."

"I don't know what they'd want with my underpants," Lucy Littlefield said, absorbed in a television-purchased book detailing exotic Oriental coming-of-age practices.

Dickie was visiting his wife, Jane, in the early recuperative stages of flu, and their child, Peter, whose own flu appeared to be in full bloom. Dickie half wanted them home in his rather done-up house on Madison Street and half didn't. He could play his Rachmaninoff

CD collection as loud as he wished, but he missed Peter's gurgles and Jane's unfussy, organizing presence.

"You're not to sell this house until you talk to me first," Dickie instructed his aunt-in-law, who was examining delicious depictions of torture gone amok with her magnifying glass.

"I'm only going to sell," Lucy said, "if they pay me twice as much as Wyn tells me it's worth." Lucy, who had come into money a few years back, had disappointed her detractors by not throwing it away on expensive froufrou.

All of her froufrou was dirt cheap and came from the home shopping channel; the money, safely invested and looked after by Wyn and Lucy's niece Jane, as coexecutors, continued to grow.

"I don't know why you're teasing Frank and his mistress-sister, then," Dickie said. "They're only going to offer you a tenth of its value."

Lucy ignored this, tut-tutting over her book.

"We're going to have to get a governor on that home shopping channel, Auntie." Dickie rinsed off the plate and cup he had been using and, air-kissing wife and baby good-bye from a safe distance, he slipped out the kitchen door, heading for his Main Street shop, ffrench's Fine Antiques. He might have stayed a moment longer but he really didn't want to deal with Frank and Merrie so early in the morning.

"You're wearing pink again," Merrie observed, straightening the magazines on the outdoor wicker table before she sat down. She couldn't stand disorder.

"It suits me," Lucy said with more hope than accuracy. "Sit. I'll get you coffee. I'd invite you in but Jane's convalescing here with Baby ffrench and they both have raging influenza."

She reappeared a few moments later with square, chipped pink cups recently purchased from the Goodwill shop and a black plastic tray piled high with supermarket cookies. After lukewarm instant coffee was dispersed, Lucy put her sharp elbows on the table and came right to the point. "How much?"

Merrie, who had been following the progress across the wicker table of a large, unidentifiable bug, and was unused to Lucy's ways, asked, "What?" in puzzlement.

"How much you want?" Frank, who had no trouble in following Lucy, shot back.

"One point two."

"One point two what?"

"One point two million dollars, American."

"Thanks, Lucy," Frank said, rising, interrupting Merrie, who was in the process of dispatching the bug with a rolled copy of *TV Guide*. "If you ever decide to visit this planetary system again, give a call."

"Too much or too little?" Lucy called after the siblings as they strode toward their sensational car.

"The fisherman's shack in Montauk," Merrie said, looking several ways before she slowly inched the Roller out Lowe Lane onto Widow Davitt's Road. Frank, who knew that Merrie meant the shack would be their next project, didn't respond. "Are you all right, brother? You look so blue."

"I was thinking of Myra and Flinty and how naive they were. Two geese waiting for the butchers. I'd like to kill all those bastards who took advantage of them." Frank let his head rest against the blood-red upholstery.

Merrie was wondering where they might lunch. Some place that would lift Frank's spirits. He had been so unhappy since Myra Stein had died. Neither time passing nor drugs taken seemed to help. Merrie's fear—

that Frank might have to go back to the equestrian sanitorium—asserted itself.

"You were a great comfort to Myra," Merrie said, deciding on the bare-bones Thai place in East Hampton. The neon orange and pink walls made him smile. She reached for his hand.

"No," Frank said, retrieving his hand, closing his eyes, looking so moony and sad that Merrie wanted to give him a little shove to make him stand up and cheer and play the game of life. "Myra was the comfort," he went on. "Her affection, those after-school all-American treats and the dumb TV movies we watched together kept me from descending into all sorts of homemade hells."

"I do wish she hadn't died in that place," Merrie said. "One would have thought her son . . ."

"LeRoy wasn't to blame, Merrie."

Merrie asked who was but Frank had slipped into one of his dangerous half naps, eyelids lowered but not quite closed. He knew quite well who was to blame.

Chapter

8

ONE OF THOSE UNEXPECTED, UNASKED-FOR STROKES OF LUCK
had descended upon Waggs Neck Harbor Realty on
Friday afternoon. A pair of Bronxville dermatologists
had fallen in love with a heretofore unsalable barn on
Lowe Lane.

The elderly owners had been wise enough to accept
the deal the moment it was offered; no contingencies
except—again wisely—that the property was being sold
in an "as is" condition.

What the skin doctors had bought, essentially, was a
nice buildable lot, prone to flooding. The dump fees for
removing the barn would be horrendous, but they were
rich and youngish and Wyn had meticulously pointed
out the rotting joists, the water-stained roof, and the
lack of code standard wiring, insulation, and town
water hookups.

"How much will you make?" Tommy asked, serving
the take-out egg drop soup, egg roll, and chow mein

at the scarred pine dining table Dickie ffrench wouldn't let Wyn have refinished lest she destroy its value.

"Six thousand simoleons. When it closes, which—cross your toes—should be next week."

"Shoes for baby." Tommy was endearingly chomping his way through the chow mein with fork and spoon, scrupulously leaving Wyn's share untouched.

"What baby?" Wyn asked, silver eyes narrowing, chow mein-bearing chopsticks halfway to mouth.

Tommy, believing he had grown wiser in the ways of marital warfare, ignored this and said, "And the good thing is nobody in the village is getting gee'd by some damn New Yorker."

" 'Gee'd' meaning 'ripped off,' Tommy?" Wyn said, eyes now at dangerous slit level, alerting Tommy he was in for *the* lecture. "If anyone got gee'd, it was the dermatologists.

"And if you're still dumb enough to believe hordes of benevolent millionaires are about to descend upon Waggs Neck Harbor and buy up the hopeless, the falling down, and the beyond repair for what the villagers consider fair value, Lord help you."

Tommy had pressed one of Wyn's more sensitive buttons. The truth of the matter was she felt on shaky ground. Recycling Victorian houses for a goodly profit was probably not one of the approved philosophic endeavors.

"The people," she went on, nonetheless, "who have bought the old wrecks that no one could afford to live in anymore and made them into potentially livable spaces have also brought you and me and the others the possibility of a livelihood. They've given us new life and sophistication and a modicum of culture.

"Instead of vilifying them and accusing them of robbery—geeing, indeed—you and me and the rest of our provincial, inbred neighbors should be on our hands and knees . . ."

"The lady doth protest too much, methinks," Tommy said, making use of his Gems of Shakespeare course at the extension college. In his heart, Tommy felt that no matter what Wyn self-servingly argued, there was something basically wrong about outsiders coming in to his village and making money out of houses that had belonged, in some cases for over a hundred years, to the families that built them.

His own mother had sold their family house to Frank and Merrie for next to nothing. Those two had made over a hundred thousand dollars on it after they dolled it up with glue-gun carpentry and Home Depot commodes.

Tommy was aware that this was a deep and maybe even damning disagreement between himself and the woman he loved and so he kept it buried most of the time. When it surfaced, he invariably slept alone in the guest room while Wyn took her solace with Probity.

Since he did not want to sleep alone tonight, he kissed her. The kiss, only about ninety percent honest, was full-bodied, full-blown, and unscrupulous. It went on for some time, evolving into their making love in the dining room surrounded by the detritus of take-out Chinese food. They might have slept there had the telephone not started to ring.

Getting into what she had so unthinkingly taken off, Wyn answered the telephone on the seventh ring. Merrie's stentorian voice came at her, sounding as if she were at the wrong end of a wind tunnel. "Merely checking, Wyn," she said.

"Checking on what, Merrie?" Wyn asked distractedly.

"Well," Merrie said, her voice becoming increasingly

British-inflected while trailing off until it was about as distinct as if they were using tin cans and a string to communicate. She was on her car phone.

"Was there anything special you wanted, Merrie?"

"I wanted to make absolutely certain tomorrow was on. We're not fooling about that fisherman's shack." Wyn said she knew that, wondering if Merrie was ever going to get to the point when she did. "You haven't by chance seen Frankie this evening, have you?"

"No," Wyn said, standing in discomfort on the dining room rug, watching a nude Tommy clear up. His rear end was well nigh perfect; his front end was a porn filmmaker's fantasy. "What?" she asked, missing Merrie's last words.

"He went for a drive in the Porsche around six, saying he needed some space. I haven't heard from him since and it's nearly nine o'clock. I took out the Roller to see if I could track him down and now I'm out here on Mill Stone Road totally discombobulated and not sure how to get home."

"Can you see the old Mill Stone Tavern?"

"I'm in the car park next to it."

"Make a left as you come out of the drive and continue until you hit West Sea Road. Don't worry about Frank. He's home, fretting about you."

"Do you really think so?"

"Try calling him on the cellular."

"I'm sure you're right," Merrie said. "Never occurred to me he might have arrived home while I was combing the countryside for him. Well, thanks so much, Winnie, for all your advice. See you on the morrow, and ta."

Wyn did not enjoy being called Winnie but she stifled her objections and made for the upstairs bath when the phone rang again. Tommy answered and shouted up that it was Frank Jones.

"Merrie called seconds ago, wondering where you were," Wyn said, taking the portable phone with her to the bath.

"I'm home. I was wondering where the hell she was. She's lived here nearly ten years and still gets lost."

"She's on her way. Why don't you call her on her cell phone and reassure her?" Wyn pushed the button that turned the ringer off, ran the bath, adding expensive French purple bubble bath (Tommy's Valentine's Day present) to the tub. She wasn't enamored of the sickly lavender aroma, which reminded her of Sen-Sen; she got in and luxuriated anyway, wondering if there was trouble in paradise, if Merrie and Frank were having a spat.

She stopped thinking about them when Tommy joined her in the tub. "It's a bit tight," Wyn said as she scooted over to make room for him.

"Hey, that's the way I like it."

The third call of the evening came when Wyn and Tommy were lying in bed, watching the final credits of *The Third Man*, Joseph Cotten sucking on a cigarette as Alida Valli walked past him and the zither ran amok riffing the theme song.

The call was from LeRoy. Tommy took it. "He sounded strange," Tommy said, hanging up, putting one arm under Wyn's head so that his biceps acted as her pillow. He smelled baby boy sweet.

"What did LeRoy want?" Wyn asked but really didn't want to know, licking his neck as if he were a lollipop.

"Quit that unless you're serious," Tommy said. "He wanted to make sure you knew about the New Federal Centennial's food committee meeting tomorrow at ten. You, him, Mike Bell, Patty Batista, and Liz, all in your office. He said it's mandatory."

All the relaxation the earlier events had brought to Wyn's tired mind and body dissolved as she grabbed the phone and punched in LeRoy's number. He either wasn't in or wasn't answering, so she told the answering machine that *nothing* was mandatory; that she was a free agent and volunteering her time; that some people did work for a living and that she was formally resigning from the food committee; and, in fact, he could take the food committee and put it where Lettie Browne reputedly stored her pearls.

The trouble with leaving incendiary messages on friends' answering machines is that, unlike unsent letters, one can't get them back. Wyn spent the next thirty minutes working for but not achieving sleep as she remembered that Myra, LeRoy's mother, had recently died. That he was out of funds and luck and was trying, pathetically, to put on a good front. That all his development dreams were just that and he was going to have to, soon, face up to the fact that he needed a mundane job. And who wanted to hire a fat man without any obvious job skills, wearing an expensive French-cuffed shirt that had seen palmier days?

"Why did you let me go on like that?" a miserable, guilt-laden Wyn asked a nearly sleeping Tommy, who smiled and said, "Huh?" She pinched him and kissed his unfurrowed brow and then the telephone rang.

Resignedly, Wyn reached for the receiver. While she fought it mightily there was no denying this aspect of her neurosis. Even on her deathbed, she knew she would answer the phone.

"I didn't wake you, did I, Wynsome?" Lettitia Browne, at her most appallingly arch, asked. "I know how you and young Tom enjoy your, uhm, beauty sleep. Clever of you to take a younger man for your second husband, Wynsome."

"Tommy and I are the same age."

"Really? One would never know."

"How may I help you, Lettie?"

"Only checking on your research progress, my dear. If you'd rather I call back, if you're in the middle of something delectable, I certainly . . ."

"The research is coming along nicely," Wyn said, wondering what would happen to her in the way of judicial punishment if she drove over to Lettie's house and punched out her lights.

Lettie was referring to a project Wyn had taken on, investigating the provenance of Lettie's New Federal Inn. It was a labor of love. Wyn, as always, was caught up in the romance and language of old deeds of sale. She had pored over the convoluted village records, damning the dim microfiche, not to mention the penmanship of long-dead village clerks.

She had found a number of photos documenting the hotel in its various incarnations from early rooming house to postwar travelers' hotel to the swank inn Lettie's late brother created and passed on to her.

Lettie had promised to publish Wyn's findings as a commemorative for the hotel's one hundredth anniversary celebration. Wyn, who liked to think she might have become a writer if not for her pride, impatience, and insecurity, was quietly pleased. She envisioned a white-kid-bound limited edition with her name discreetly printed in gold on the cover. Not merely a souvenir pamphlet but an instructive and witty bit of prose to be savored long after the moment passed.

"Marvelous," Lettie was saying. "To switch gears, Wynsome, did you by any chance attend the late late aerobics class at the Spa?"

Wyn, who tried but rarely managed to show up for

Patty Batista's demanding classes at the Old Railroad Station Spa, asked why.

"I was wondering if you saw Mike Bell there. He's moonlighting as the Spa night manager and he doesn't seem to have come back to the inn after the Spa closed. Not that I'm his keeper . . ."

Oh, yeah, Wyn thought but didn't say.

". . . but we do need the keys to lock the wine cellar and he doesn't seem to have left them. Anywhere."

This was pathetically weak and even Lettie's trained, nicely modulated voice couldn't carry it off. Oh, Lord, Wyn thought. Poor Lettie. She's starring in one of her plays: the rich, older woman in lust with the impecunious younger hunk. *The Roman Spring of Mrs. Stone? Chéri? The Last of Chéri?* Wyn felt a burst of sympathy for Lettie, who didn't deserve it, and said, "No, I haven't been near the Spa all week."

"Doesn't matter, really, does it?" Lettie allowed a note of despair to creep into her throaty delivery, seemingly unwilling to end the conversation. "You know Mike. Such a free spirit under that hair and muscle. Oh, well. He probably was exhausted dealing with all those hens and fell asleep on one of the workout mats. I'll ring off now and talk to you very soon, Wynsome, darling."

If Mike Bell had fallen asleep on one of Patty Batista's greasy workout mats, Wyn was prepared to eat one. At least if he fell asleep alone.

Wyn's thought that Mike Bell was nothing if not a lady-killer led to exactly the ghost she had been trying to keep at bay as Petronella's unlovely visage swam into the TV tube in her mind.

Chapter

9

ORDINARILY, WYN WOULD HAVE WELCOMED A DRIVE TO Montauk with Frank and Merrie in the Rolls-Royce on a bright spring Saturday morning. The lilacs were knocking themselves out with fragrance and yard sales were transforming the rural stretches of the highway into an endless bazaar. And Wyn knew that she was sure to be entertained by Frank's dark, thin wit and Merrie's obtuse observations.

But the early morning hadn't gone well and Wyn, though she wouldn't admit it, was a touch cranky. To start with, when she arrived at her office at eight A.M., Pasko was waiting on the bench outside, looking like a starved meat eater gearing up for a beef bacchanal. He had on his tight gabardine suit, scrupulously shined black lace-ups, and a Steve McQueen scowl.

"Howdy," he said, standing up. I'm the rain cloud, he thought, uncharacteristically poetic, surprising himself. She's the sun.

Wyn, who had not foreseen Pasko on her doorstep, tried—out of mere mother-bred politeness—to keep her expression neutral as she unlocked the door of Waggs Neck Harbor Realty and disarmed the alarm system. She wished she had come in through the parking lot entry. She would have liked a little time before dealing with Pasko.

Maybe it was the dimple in his chin that looked surgically placed. Maybe it was the lone wolf air he wore as comfortably as he did his down-market clothes. Against her will, Wyn felt a pang of pity for the detective when what she wanted was not to know him at all.

He followed her into her office as she flicked on lights, opened blinds, and found the report she had promised him. Wyn stayed upright, hoping he would take his report and his little blue cloud and move on. But he chose the green leather visitor's chair, sitting with his elbows on his knees, putting extra stress on his suit seams as he scanned the list Liz Lum had assembled.

Wyn gave up and, emitting a theatrical sigh, sat behind her father's father's partners desk and waited. Concentrating on the report, Pasko unconsciously unbuttoned his jacket and Wyn caught a glimpse of a gun stashed in a holster strapped under his arm.

He saw revulsion altering her usual poker face. "It ain't my private parts," he said, adjusting the holster.

Wyn wasn't so certain. She found the fact sheet on the Montauk fisherman's cottage Merrie and Frank were so hot for and attempted to concentrate on such facts as square footage, air-conditionable space, and legal right of way.

Pasko stood up. Now she wished he'd sit down. She didn't like him hovering over her. But for once he wasn't appraising her like a gourmand peregrine picking out the plumpest pheasant. He was collating the notes in his hand with the red flags in his mind, detailing the intricacies of the Bell duck farm deal, that complex, multistaged realty transaction deal on which Wyn and Petronella St. Cloud and a woman named Kathleen Carruthers and, yes, those two long-ago strangled female attorneys—McFee and Leverage—had worked together.

"Who's Kathleen Carruthers?" he asked, after a few moments, knowing but wanting Wyn's take.

"A Realtor based in Montauk. Coincidentally, I'm seeing her later this morning."

"She works Waggs Neck Harbor, too?"

"And Southampton. Carrutherses have been here forever, up and down the South Fork. Kathy has her fingers in any number of real estate pies. Those Waggs Neckers who don't trust me use her."

"Tell her I want to see her later."

"Tell her yourself."

"What's her number?" Pasko asked, feeling ill-used.

"You'll find it in the Montauk directory."

"You know, you're not very nice to me," Pasko said with a boy's sense of unfairness as he got up and left.

For a moment, Wyn was ashamed. She *wasn't* very nice to him and she wasn't certain why. Nonetheless, she was pleased to see his muscular back, telling herself she'd have to learn to be civil to him. Both her parents had taught her that civility rules.

Not long after, the Rolls pulled up and Merrie gave a quick rooty-toot-toot of the clarion horn.

Wyn indicated she was coming, taking a moment to call Kathy's office as a double check. Kathy's cheery answering tape was on but no home number was supplied. I suppose she's going straight to the property, Wyn hoped. She didn't relish the thought of schlepping out to the end of Long Island only to find that Kathy was that Realtors' demon, a no-show.

Wyn had long had a suspicion that Kathleen Carruthers was one of those women born fully formed at the age of fifty-three. She wore her gray and brown hair in a messy upsweep held together by a worm-colored rubber band; she looked down upon makeup and clothes that fit.

She had been a hipper-than-thou flower child during the correct decade and never let anyone forget it. "No drugs," she liked to say in her gushy voice. "Just love, love, love."

A rich fisherman's daughter and a rich fisherman's childless wife—both fellows now deceased—she was sometimes a touch overcommitted to her calling. She had proved this once when showing Wyn and her clients—a meek pharmacist and his mustachioed wife—a Montauk condo. There had been no answer at the door and the key Kathy had didn't work.

Kathy had muttered, somewhat meaninglessly, "Oh well, in for a pound," and used her ungloved hand to smash the door's window to gain entry. An alarm went off. The pharmacist and wife fled, Wyn not far behind. "Turned out it was the wrong apartment. They made me replace the glass," Kathy reported later, aggrieved.

Not surprisingly, Kathy Carruthers was a multimillion-home seller, the kind of Realtor featured in national real estate magazine stories, a welcome guest lecturer at Prudential Realty national seminars.

The bird-nest hair, the unfettered and mammoth mammary glands beneath black turtleneck sweaters, the alarmingly large derriere under big gal blue jeans . . . all this was exactly what the tired upper working class were looking for when they were weekend cottage hunting in Montauk. No glamour, no chic, just down-home, straight-from-the-shoulder talk about the glories of living at the eastern end of the South Fork, surrounded by water and sky and sand and the likes of Kathy Carruthers.

Wyn cringed whenever she had to do business with her. Genuine country women were difficult enough; Barnard-educated Kathleen ("You call me Kathy, honey") was beyond the pale.

Stifling her pessimism, Wyn slid into the luxurious passenger seat next to Merrie. She had to assume that Kathy would turn up; that she was hip enough to realize that Merrie and Frank, having given up on Waggs Neck, might be the bread and butter of her golden years. Wyn had no qualms about setting Merrie and Frank onto Montauk and Kathy Carruthers. Somehow a gentrified—or Merrified—Montauk didn't seem so terrible to Wyn.

"Now would someone please tell me," Merrie said as her leviathan shot up Washington Street on their way out of Waggs Neck, "why in God's name those people don't fix up that homely little house and tend to that pathetic weed garden?" She was pointing to an oddly sited, brown-shingled abode that had had an unfortunate cinder block garage added to it in the pre-code days of the 1950s.

"They have no money, Merrie. Remember? He's out of work. She's bone lazy." Frank sprawled in the back seat, oversized white sunglasses making him look as if he had gone Hollywood. He was so pale and blue skinned, Wyn found herself worrying about his health.

"Then they should sell it to us," Merrie persisted. "We were very fair in our offer but would they listen to reason? No, they would not. Now I hope they're good and sorry because I wouldn't take it if they gave it to us."

Clients who attempted to purchase houses without the advice and experience of a bona fide Realtor (and the commission due) made Wyn's blood run hot and cold, though she kept her counsel. There were few houses Merrie and Frank were going to be able to buy without a Realtor; their raptor reputation was the theme of too many East End cautionary tales.

"Are you up to this?" Wyn asked Frank, changing subjects, having had enough of what Merrie felt the downtrodden of the world owed her.

"I'm fine, Wyn," Frank said, although he appeared to be headed for the last roundup in his boots and leather vest.

They drew abreast of a heavily advertised three-family yard sale and Merrie insisted on stopping. "There's going to be no bargaining," Frank predicted, coming to life a bit. Wyn wondered if the glue in their relationship was their shared blood lust for bargains large and small.

"Not after they've spotted the Roller there won't," Merrie agreed, launching herself out of the car, warming to her task. "Maybe," Merrie went on, leading the way, "we should get ourselves a Dodge for yard sailing."

Frank was amused by this suggestion. "Merrie is a trip," he said to no one in particular, as he headed for a bolt of what might have been hand-printed silk.

Wyn watched Frank pick his way from folding table to folding table. He moved so nicely and that strange coppery coloring gave him a seductive otherworldly air. He was like the boy in "Death in Venice." Any number of lonely people could easily fall in love with him.

Merrie checked the diamond and gold Victorian lapel watch she had inherited from her aunt Flo and snorted. "We'd better get a move on, hadn't we?" she asked, looking at Wyn as if she were the cause of their tardiness. "We don't want to keep the Carruthers person waiting."

Chapter

10

⁂

THE VISTA ABRUPTLY CHANGED AS THEY LEFT AMAGANSETT, becoming more beach resort, less country village. Terraced acres of ill-proportioned A-frames and dome houses squatted obscenely beside one another, jostling for a view of the beach.

Stretches of Long Island Sound followed, interspersed with diners and small businesses connected with the sea. "It's like the world's longest tongue depressor out here," Merrie commented. "The sound on your left, the ocean on your right. One can only wonder where the developers have been."

"They're here now," Wyn said brightly.

Merrie gave her a sharp look. And then, wrongly deciding it was an innocent comment, said: "Well, we're going to start small and then we'll see. Right, Brother Frank?"

"Right, Sister Merrie."

As they approached Montauk, Merrie took the old

highway, which skirted the Atlantic Ocean. Undistin-
guished houses, ranches and split levels, reminiscent of
the Eisenhower years, sat above and below the road.
They suited the stark landscape, far more elemental
here than back in cozy Waggs Neck Harbor, which
Wyn suddenly, absurdly, missed.

"Thar she blows," Merrie said, after several miles of
sobering seascape. Fairly isolated, the small house sat
to the left of the old two-lane highway and was reached
by what appeared to be a nearly perpendicular driveway. Built of weathered board and batting, it was unre-
markable except for its site: a quarter of an acre of
sandy knoll with an unobstructed view of the beach
and the ocean. "A multimillion-dollar view," Merrie
said, parking the Rolls at a sharp incline, stepping out
on the brick driveway. "And a ten-thousand-dollar
house."

Wyn agreed, thinking it looked ripe for Frank and
Merrie's brand of renovation although they'd have to
be careful not to make it look like a motel unit.

Moving up the hill with gusto, Merrie seemed already sold. "We'll have to privatize like mad but the
pool can be petite. Possibilities galore. Right, Frankie?"

Frank said, again, right, Merrie. He stood by the car
for a moment with Wyn. "She's nuts, you know," Frank
said. "I mean I'm crazy and you're marginally insane
but we both know, deep down, we're lunatics.

"Merrie hasn't a clue. She thinks she's perfectly logical and rational and everyone else isn't. How I'd like
to get inside that head for a moment and see what's
really going on."

He walked up the steep hill, joining Merrie on the
deck. He put his arm in hers. "It's splendid," he said,
looking at the sea, smiling. "Where is Ms. Carruthers?"

Wyn was wondering the same thing. Using the cellular phone, she called Kathy's office. Marge, her space cadet of a secretary—all that THC in the sixties—said she was out. Wyn said, really, where was she? Marge said she'd have to look in the book and Wyn said why didn't she do that.

"Look, can I get back to you?"

"No," Wyn said coldly.

With time and patience, she elicited the information that the last entry in the book indicated that Kathy was showing the Fisher house. Or maybe she was showing a person named Fisher a house. "Her handwriting," Marge said lamely. "Oh, wait."

"What?" Wyn said, teeth gridlocked.

"You know what? I think this Fisher entry may be for yesterday afternoon," Marge said without a great deal of confidence. "There's no telling with her handwriting . . . though I'm ninety percent sure this says the Fisher house . . ."

Wyn downloaded Marge with a flip of the cellular and looked up to find the deck empty. "The door was unlocked," Merrie called out to her. "Come in, it's darling."

Wyn, who remained on the deck, said she wasn't risking her license no matter how darling it was and that she was going to walk up the beach to see if Kathy was at the Fisher house.

"Do," Merrie said, so transparently delighted to get rid of her that Wyn laughed.

"Take the car," Frank said through the window Merrie was opening, as he settled into a once-white bean-bag chair.

Wyn, who did not like driving other people's Rolls-Royces, lied and said it would be faster if she walked.

* * *

Leaving her shoes behind, Wyn crossed the road and took the wooden stairs that led over the dunes and the sea grass and the various weedlike plants the environmentalists had optimistically planted as erosion insurance. She spent a moment looking across the wide expanse of white sand to the calm, gray-blue waters of the Atlantic.

Then, feeling she had done her contemplative duty for the day, she marched on, enjoying the feeling of sand between her toes, hoping incontinent dogs had not been there before her. Frank and Merrie, she knew, would be nicely occupied for hours, planning the new kitchen and the outdoor glass brick shower.

As she walked on the water side of the dunes, enjoying the nippy breeze and the solitude, feeling as fancy-free as an actress in a feminine hygiene commercial, her mind returned to its favorite subject: real estate.

It would be a coup if Kathy could sell Carl Fisher's old Mediterranean monstrosity. Fisher, who made a fortune developing Miami Beach in the 1920s, lost it attempting to do the same to Montauk a decade later.

Wyn found the rickety stairs that led up to the Fisher house and marveled again at the monstrous phallic red-brick turrets sticking up here and there around the house. The soaring tiled roofs and the multiplicity of French doors giving out onto piazzas and loggias and Mussolini balconies evoked the worst of Mizner's Balkanized Palm Beach palazzi. Wyn made her way up and down several levels and along what seemed like miles of brick terrace to the gargantuan front door on the second tier.

The place appeared deserted. Wyn had a feeling that Kathy Carruthers was not here and was not going to turn up either. Didn't matter, after all. Merrie and Frank had gotten into the property they wanted; negotiation could be carried on via telephone and fax. Probably better that Kathy had stayed away. Her Granny Dumpling style was not really suited to Frank's Blue Boy impersonation or Merrie's Lady Astor turn.

She knocked on the door just because she thought she should and gave half a shout when it swung open as if Boris Karloff were on the other side. "Doesn't anyone lock the doors of empty houses in Montauk?" Wyn asked no one in particular as she reached in across the threshold to grab the wrought-iron handle to close the door.

That's when she spotted Kathy's green canvas Gap carryall in the far corner of the chapel-like foyer. "Oh, no," Wyn said, stepping in, hating the shaky feeling in her bones.

Kathy Carruthers was lying face up in front of a mammoth stone fireplace adorned with concrete griffins and snakes. Her bunioned feet were encased in yellow plastic jelly sandals; her thick red neck was wrapped in navy-blue panty hose; her surprisingly elegant hands were folded across her considerable waist. All very tidy.

A pervasive odor combined with the unthinkable caused Wyn to make for the door, the terrace, and the salty air. She sat on a sun-warmed brick half-wall and put her head between her knees. Eventually she was able to sit up and get the cell phone from the pocket in which it was lodged. Her fingers shook and her tongue felt like the Sahara at noon in July.

She badly wanted to call her dad but he was dead. Then she wanted to call Tommy, but enough, she told herself, was enough. She was supposed to be a big, liberated girl; finding strangled Realtors was becoming a commonplace. Her responsibility was to call the police in the person of Detective Pasko.

As so often before when she knew what she was supposed to do, Wyn did what she wanted to do. Instead of ringing up Pasko, she found herself calling a policeman she trusted: Homer Price.

Chapter

11

Unlike Wyn, Captain Homer Price, Waggs Neck Harbor Police Chief, knew immediately who he had to call. But he didn't do so until he was in his gleaming black-and-blue police cruiser, siren blaring, taking the back roads at sound-barrier speed, destination Montauk.

"You can stay out of this," Pasko said, as if he were doing Homer a favor.

"I'm halfway there."

"Yo, Spud," Pasko said, getting into his jacket while juggling his cell phone, checking his standard issue revolver as he raced down the metal stairs of the West Sea headquarters, "like this is big-time shit. You stick to incarcerating jaywalkers and town drunks."

Homer did what the police academy biofeedback instructor had suggested and took a deep inhalation before responding. "You want to stop everything right here and now," he said evenly, "and let the Montauk police handle this while we get a clarification of our orders from your chief and our senator? As I understand it, we're to work together."

"And right you are, Spud, but . . ."

". . . don't call me 'Spud,' Detective. Or any other belittling names . . ."

"Hey, Dude, like I'm sorry. Don't want to mess with your sensitivities. You want to go by the book, Captain Midnight, we will go by the book."

" 'Midnight' is another pejorative," Homer said with what seemed like infinite patience though his hands were clutching the steering wheel as if it were Pasko's neck. "A racist pejorative, at that."

"I thought everyone in the village called you 'Midnight.' My apologies, again, Captain Price." Pasko was doing ninety up crooked, potholed West Sea Road. "Just do me a favor. Like if you get there first, don't fuck up the crime scene, *comprende,* Bro?"

Their hatred was the kind that raised hairs on the backs of necks, the basic, primeval, instant detestation that Pasko believed made men men.

Not that each reacted in the same way. The more street-mean Pasko turned, the more civilized, cultivated, and college-bred Homer became. Five-foot-nine Pasko, in his wise-guy suit, with his fallen angel's face and sour energy was a film noir detective. Homer Price, six foot three with shoulders that wouldn't stop and thick bulges in all the right places, possessed a noble, handsome head in the new, Afro-American telegenic style. They were as opposite as if they came from different media.

At their first meeting, Homer had not moved from his well-kept desk when Pasko had exploded in through the door. He had remained seated, huge hands folded prayerlike behind the brass pen and pencil set, a fifty-four-inch-square autographed photo portrait of Ronald Reagan behind him.

Continuing to dictate a letter to his rainbow-haired secretary, Yolanda, he had given no sign of recognition as Pasko stood steaming in the center of the room barely taking in the tan linoleum floor and the recently painted industrial green walls.

"One chief, huh?" Pasko finally said. "Not so many Indians."

Homer dictated on. The letter was to the mayoress about the inadvisability of locking up suspect high school marijuana smokers without catching them in the act; hearsay via her niece wasn't enough.

He finished and looked up but not at Pasko. "Yolanda, escort this gentleman outside and find out what he wants and who he is. If he needs to make an appointment, look at early next week."

"You know goddamn well who I am and what I want, Captain. So here's how it's going to work. You keep out of it and if and when I solve this fucker, I'll tell everyone you were like real helpful."

"I don't think so," Homer said as Pasko was halfway out the door.

"You know what happens when you guys think."

"Racist bastard," Homer said, as the door shut and its pebbly green glass shook. "All Polacks are."

Yolanda knew her boss well enough not to point out the irony of his statement. But she couldn't resist saying, "That's one hot Polack racist, you gotta give him credit. Like I wouldn't mind nabbing a bit of that myself."

At first glance it looked like a successful spring garden party, chatty attendees standing in relaxed groups on the sunny second-level entry terrace of Carl Fisher's old Montauk monument to architectural kitsch.

Gathered together were several white-overalled and totally bored members of the crime scene team from Riverhead, waiting with their minivacuums and tweezers and plastic gloves for Pasko to give them the go-ahead. Also present were the medical examiner's boisterous golf partner, who decided to come along because he had nothing else to do and had always wanted to see the Fisher house; various stout members of the Montauk police force drinking iced coffee from plastic cups; Kathleen Carruthers's secretary, weepy though her thick kohl eye makeup remained intact; three of Kathy Carruthers's local cousins looking thoughtful, fantasizing about the will; and Wyn and her clients.

Merrie and Frank, worried about Wyn's long absence, had driven over, parking the Rolls in such a haphazard fashion that no other car could get up the steep driveway that led to the baronial stairs, which in turn led to the second-floor main entry.

Merrie had made a fuss when Homer arrived and demanded she move the car. "Public officials have no manners in this country. You'd think he'd offer to move it for me. But no, I have to trudge down those steps . . ."

The rest of her complaint was lost in the wind but she had more to say when she returned, having thought through the repercussions of Kathy's murder. "Does this mean we're going to have trouble getting our hands on the cottage?" she wanted to know, as she sat down next to Wyn on a stone bench, taking her cold hand, holding it between her warm ones. The gesture was surprisingly comforting.

"Merrie, stop," Frank said.

"Merely being pragmatic, dearie."

Pasko, followed by Homer and the medical examiner, finally exited the house, giving the signal for the crime scene team to swarm in. To a tune of total and sudden silence, a pair of spaghetti-thin men rolled out a glistening chrome gurney, bearing what was presumably Kathy Carruthers wrapped in a sealed body bag.

This noiseless pavane stopped for a moment as the leading Carruthers cousin said, "When can we have her?"

The ME, lighting a cigarette inserted into an elegant FDR holder, said the family would be contacted and turned the cousins over to a policewoman, who was to take their statements.

"We got to stop meeting like this," Pasko said, coming up to Wyn, eyeing Merrie and Frank. "What are you two doing here?" he asked, not liking Frank's signet ring nor the outrage on Merrie's face.

"Before we give you that information," Merrie said in her Queen Mother way, "may I inquire what *you* are doing here, Sergeant Pasko? I thought Montauk was out of your district."

As Pasko disabused Merrie of her wrong notions, Wyn retired to the far corner of the terrace and spoke dejectedly to Homer. Pasko followed her progress as he half listened to Merrie protest the indignity of not being allowed to leave.

"Where you going?" Pasko asked Homer and Wyn, who were about to descend the stone stairwell that led to the Waggs Neck Harbor Police Department's sole squad car. "I got some questions for Mrs. Handwerk."

"I will be taking her statement, Detective," Homer said. "You want to read it, call me later at my office."

Pasko visibly restrained himself, an effort that caused several blue veins in his neck to pulsate and his eyes to bulge unpleasantly.

By the time Pasko gauged himself able to speak in his normal voice, Homer was helping a still barefoot Wyn into his car. She had put on black Jackie O. shades and from Pasko's overhead view, she looked like a slain leader's tragic widow. Given what he was putting together, he hoped she wasn't going to be slain herself.

He shook himself out of his Wyn Lewis daydream and looked around the terrace. As far as he could tell, the only citizens worth talking to were the bizarro brother and sister act and that loon of a secretary from the Carruthers office. He'd get them on tape and then take a quick trip into Waggs Neck, where he'd get some pleasure out of scaring the bejesus out of Ms. Wynsome Lewis, Realtor, attorney, and current reigning star of his fantasy life.

He wished to God that he could stop thinking about her. He thought he might be more worried for her than she was. He hadn't been able to tell from her face or body language whether or not she was scared. Underneath all the clicking and clacking going on in his brain was the lubricant of alarm. Hers was the last name on the computer list Cora had generated for him:

Penny McFee
Harriet Leverage
Petronella St. Cloud
Kathy Carruthers
Wyn Lewis

Chapter
12

It was barely eight-thirty and Wyn was already Monday-morninged out. Liz brought her coffee in her least favorite mug, the one with the handle in the guise of an improbably colored penguin.

Liz Lum's penguin fetish was out of control again, seeping out of her domain, inexorably taking over the front room in the form of a plastic penguin umbrella stand and creeping into Wyn's office where a new, smiley glass penguin pencil holder had appeared on her desk. It would stay there, Wyn decided, until some clumsy person like herself knocked it off.

"Have you thought of talking to someone about the penguins?" Wyn asked—and not for the first time—but Liz wasn't listening. She was curled up like a question mark in the green chair, downing coffee like a trucker, reciting the litany of woes brought on her by her daughter.

"Heidi's still dating Dax Fiori, which is fine, I suppose.

I mean he's going to Dartmouth on a Merit Scholarship. Dax clearly has a future; can't argue with that. But Heidi's seeing Mike Bell on the QT . . ."

"How do you know?" Wyn, though she often told herself she shouldn't, relished village dish.

"I listen in on the extension. Of course this is between you, me, and the lamppost because if Lettie Browne ever found out, she'd have Miss Heidi for breakfast."

"Don't underestimate our Heidi."

"You don't suppose Heidi's having sex with Mike Bell, do you, Wyn?"

"You don't suppose she's not. Mike Bell isn't the kind of guy who has bought heavily into the concept of pure and romantic love."

"Do you think she's sleeping with Dax, too?" Liz was starting to grope in her red denim overall pocket for her hankie.

"It's a possibility," Wyn said. Then she saw the expression on her friend's long, olive-complected face and tried to think of something reassuring to say but couldn't.

She sighed and went back to the study of the plot map for Merrie and Frank's potential new project. As was often the case with this kind of property—old and much traded—there were ancient encroachments and potentially illegal rights of way that had to be investigated and dealt with.

The current owner had already enlisted a new Realtor, which didn't seem quite nice; the new Realtor had already faxed Wyn a number of documents that Merrie had requested; this, too, wasn't done.

Merrie should have been talking to just one Realtor and that was her own, Ms. Wynsome Lewis. Added to the group who seemed to lack a certain feeling for both the newly dead and the hallowed rules of realty were Kathy's cousins. They had already sought the advice of an attorney, who had just contacted Wyn as to the possibility of Kathy's estate receiving a percentage of the commission if the property were sold.

Wyn found herself yet again agreeing with Miss Marple as to the depravity of the human race, thinking that nowhere was it better demonstrated than in the commerce known as real estate.

"Dear heart, am I interrupting anything too, too important?" Lettitia Browne sailed into the office wearing a vintage tan and white Chanel spring suit that even Wyn and Liz, a pair of fashion illiterates, recognized as the genuine goods. The wide-brimmed hat and the tan and white Maude Frizzon spectator pumps gave her a considerable air of insouciance if not youth.

Liz gathered up her penguin mug and fled. Lettie always treated her as if she were an out-of-line member of the underprivileged class, and Liz invariably reacted accordingly.

"You're looking sporty today, Lettie," Wyn said. There were moments when she really disliked Lettie but there was never a time when Wyn wasn't interested in what she was about.

"I'm feeling bright and cheerful," Lettie confessed, taking Liz's vacated chair. "The weather. But you, on the other hand, look like the victim of serious *mal de mer.* Too terrible about Kathy what's-her-name; however, there it is.

"But let's not discuss dreary topics this morning, Wynsome. Do tell me how you're getting along with the history of my modest inn? I was wondering if we could sell it to *Travel & Leisure* or maybe *The New Yorker.* You're making it appropriately punchy and literary, I hope? You don't have to be totally factual, you know. James Fenimore Cooper might well have written a Natty Bumppo story in the dining room. Who's to say? And I heard a rumor that during the war Norman and Jim spent time bullshitting in the bar . . ."

"Norman and Jim? Bullshitting?"

"You are obtuse, Wynsome. Norman Mailer and James Jones. Then of course there's no reason not to work John Steinbeck in. I mean the divine Elaine comes for dinner all the time . . ."

If names routinely dropped were roles played, Lettie would have been through the entire English language drama canon twice over by this time, Wyn thought as she let her ramble on. She was dreading the ten A.M. meeting in Homer's office with himself, herself, and the redoubtable Detective Pasko. Skulking around the outer limits of her consciousness was the possibility that she was *numero uno* on some maniac's hit parade.

"You're not listening to a word I say," Lettie said. "I don't care. Neither am I. I'm distracted. I suppose I might as well confess to you . . ."

"Please don't."

". . . that I'm in lust."

"Mike Bell."

"All that heavenly hair. Everywhere. Unclad, he looks like a Kodiak bear. Oh, Wynsome, he makes me feel so young."

"Like spring is sprung. Where was he the other night when you had mislaid him, so to speak?"

"Asleep in his bed. I am besotted. I never thought to look there, of all places."

"He probably doesn't frequent it all that much. Marriage bells in our future?" Wyn asked, picking up Lettie's infectious drawing room comedy cadence.

From under the lovely hat, Lettie gave Wyn the sloe-eyed look she had used to such effect in a summer production of *Witness for the Prosecution*. "Maybe in his. I'll be over it in a few months and if he's lucky, he can hold on to his job. Oh, I know what he's thinking: marriage to me and all his problems—meaning the down-island usurer he's in hock to up to his testes—will be finis and he'll be living the life of Riley as Mr. Lettitia Browne.

"I think not. I may be in the throes of early middle-aged sexual fervor but I am not completely off my rocker. Now I must be on my way. I'm going to Southampton to let that eerie hair burner rearrange my tresses." She stood up and carefully put on her exquisite lace and suede gloves, one finger at a time.

Wyn, not quite certain what this visit had been all about—Lettie rarely did anything without a purpose—told Liz she was leaving and where she would be. She promised on her word of honor to keep her cell phone on in the event anyone had to talk to her. This was a bone of contention between the two of them, since Wyn often forgot to switch it on.

Wishing she could trade the phone for a pair of lace and suede gloves and the guts to wear them, Wyn slowly walked the few yards up Main Street toward Homer's office in the Municipal Building as if it were the last mile. She didn't like living in fear.

Dickie ffrench was leaving the Municipal Building. His saturnine face, sporting a new pair of lively poison-green glasses, didn't look happy. "Every time I turn around, they want another license. License to sell. License to buy. I tell you, Wyn, they're bleeding me dry. Now what's this I hear about Merrie and Frank moving their operation to Montauk?"

Though born and bred in Waggs Neck Harbor, Wyn could still be left breathless by the speed of the village hotline. "Merrie and Frank are not moving their operation, Dickie. They're only looking at property in Montauk."

"Where poor Kathy Carruthers met hers with a pair of

panty hose? Well, I'm glad Merrie and Frank are not giving up on our humble village. The purchasers of their glue-and-tack redos invariably prove to be superb customers. So trusting.

"Now you mustn't keep me unless you have a burning desire to waste the morning at Baby's over tea and dish. Oh, Lord, there's LeRoy Stein. What could he be wearing on his feet?"

Wyn smiled at LeRoy as he strode up Main Street in battered, elegant riding boots; he lifted two fingers to her in a rakish salute.

Wyn said no to tea. She had an appointment. Dickie asked with whom and Wyn said given the extraordinary efficiency of village communications, he'd know soon enough.

She was surprised he hadn't heard rumors about her being next on the strangler's hit list and wondered if he'd cry at her funeral.

Underneath this frivolous thought, Wyn was genuinely worried. For the first time ever, she found herself scanning the faces of Main Street, looking for who or what she wasn't certain. That was the problem.

Chapter

13

IN HIS THIGH-HIGH HUNGARIAN HUNTING BOOTS, LEROY
Stein was the envy of every dominatrix in the village.

In one part of his compartmentalized mind, he believed he was strutting along in his father's foot-
steps. Never mind that his father had died long ago.
LeRoy had early on built an image of his long-dead
dad that he held on to for dear life. In his fantasy,
Stein, Sr., had been a rakish member of the lesser
Middle Europa nobility, a Rumanian Scarlet Pimper-
nel, who had fled the Nazis but only after dispatching
a goodly number of them and after he himself had
suffered the unmentionable tortures that had broken
his health.

In reality, Stein, Sr., had been a sickly postwar refu-
gee, a Displaced Person who had turned up in Waggs
Neck Harbor in early 1945 thanks to a government-
sponsored DP-dispersal program. That he had managed
to talk Myra Fiske, the richest girl in the village, into

marrying him was a tribute to his prewar salesman's skills.

Myra had never challenged LeRoy's grandiose vision of his father, so LeRoy had grown up feeling it was his obligation to set a high European tone for the village. To that end, on this morning's stroll he sported a rakish walking stick and the kind of animal print ascot once sold at the old Abercrombie & Fitch.

Bestowing a smile on one and all, high and low, he paused just once. This was at the western end of the New Federal Inn, where Lettie had recently installed a handsome brass plaque providing the casual passerby with the history of her hostelry. LeRoy's cheeks turned red when he saw that it bore no mention of his mother's family name. If it hadn't been for the Fiskes, there would be no New Federal Inn. He was not only a Hungarian-American prince, he was, thanks to the Fiskes, a Yankee merchant prince as well but people like Lettie tended to forget that.

He strode on, his smile less benign, ending up in the old section of the cemetery. Leaning against one of the ancient oaks whose leafy branches now sheltered his mother's final resting place, he tried to think positive thoughts, as that woman would have counseled.

But he couldn't ignore the negative images of all those who had had a moral obligation to help Myra Fiske Stein through those final, horrific years of her life, and hadn't.

The guilty included those Waggs Neck Harborites whom he held responsible for the family bankruptcy under Myra's admittedly ditzy stewardship. Mismanagement or not, the sharks had had a feeding frenzy over the duck farm fiasco, taking everything, relegating Myra to the Bide-a-Wee and LeRoy to Lettie's inconsistent string-entwined subsidy-loans.

Even after he learned that Frank Jones had quietly arranged for special private accommodations for Myra, LeRoy pretended not to know; he continued to believe that the entire village had turned their fat-laden backs on Myra Fiske Stein and her son.

He felt an unexpected, intense need to be with his mother again; without warning, he began to cry as the tragedy of that woman's life, and his own, overwhelmed him. Trying to catch his breath, sobbing like an abandoned child, he pushed his butcher's fists against his eyes as if he were trying to push the tears back in.

LeRoy Stein numbered himself among those who live lives of quiet desperation. Increasingly, he felt the urge to explode.

Coincidentally, Frank Jones was making a similar sentimental hegira that Monday morning, visiting the corner of Bay Street and Widow Davitt's Road. The village, the township, the county, and the state had employed various forms of persuasion—legal and otherwise—to move him to clear the acre or so of rusting Kelvinator refrigerators, tubeless Dumont and Crosby TVs, nesting Big Mac truck tires, a pair of postwar AirStreams, and various broken/outmoded sports, kitchen, bathroom, and farming equipment. But Frank had Merrie's attorneys on his side and the phrase "grandfathered in" invariably won the day. The debris continued to lie piled in pyramidical formations above which swung the faded metal sign that still read JONES JUNQUE.

Lately there had been a reactionary movement afoot to declare Jones Junque a village landmark. Frank appreciated cheap irony as much as the next cynic but this was not what he wanted. What he wanted was to rub the village's collective proboscis into Flinty Jones's junk: the junk they had tried so hard to get rid of, the junk they themselves had largely manufactured.

But *The New York Times* "Arts & Leisure" section had done a laudatory piece on the junkyard and shortly thereafter the Manhattan Museum of Contemporary Folk Art had expressed, in a carefully worded letter, the possibility of "acquiring" part or all of the collection. Frank, who rarely laughed, did so on reading it, while Merrie wondered what was so damn funny. "These museum johnnies are serious money, Frankie."

Encouraged by the *Times* article, the Art and Historical Society began Sunday walking tours around the junkyard's perimeter. On the far side of the accordion wire-topped chain link fence, enthusiastic guides extolled "the innate creativity that had caused that eccentric genius, Flinty Jones, to amass this world-class collection of stunning, contemporary artifacts."

No one besides Frank was allowed in with the exception of the monthly exterminator (some obeisance had to be made to the public health officials' concern about rats and vermin) and the Nervous Nell of an insurance adjuster who insisted the premiums be raised to historic heights.

Flinty, who like his son had been no great shakes of a laugher, would certainly have chuckled at these first steps in elevating him into the ranks of art sainthood.

The brightness of the late April morning reflecting off the various eroding metals half blinded Frank for a moment. He walked under the eaves of the corrugated metal shack that had served as his home and the junkyard's office for so many years. Its Toonerville Trolley-esque smokestack, poking through the tin roof, seemed especially poignant, reminding him of chilly winter evenings.

The main room in the shack had been his father's office, a place in which Flinty had been happy smoking stinking black cigars, dreaming of "big" money.

There had been moments when Frank had been happy, too, sitting on a salvaged trundle bed, listening to his dad plan out loud in his odd Highland English as he dealt himself a complicated solitaire. "Real estate, laddie. That's the answer. Aye, we make a bit of money with the junk but one of these fine days Mrs. Stein is going to cut us in on a big land development deal and we're going to be so rich, money will be growing out of our noses."

Myra sure cut them in, all right, Frank thought. Not that he could blame Myra; she had thought she was inviolate, the natural heir to the Fiske fortunes. The two of them, Myra and Flinty, had been juicy red plums, ripe, as Merrie said, for the picking.

Now, inhaling with relish the specific rusty odor of decomposing metals, Frank remembered without wanting to the November day in 1987 when he and Merrie had driven out from Manhattan in answer to Wyn's warning about Flinty's depression.

Merrie had been the one to cut Flinty down and try various doomed reviving techniques; Frank had sat cross-legged on the trundle bed, staring with unwavering concentration at the beam from which Flinty had hanged himself.

The carefully scripted note said he was tired of Francis and Merredith supporting him; his health wasn't getting any better and neither were his prospects and since Mrs. Stein went into the Bide-a-Wee, he had no one to talk to. He felt it was right that Francis and

Merredith were together and his last thoughts were filled with love for his son. Though he hadn't been good at saying it, everything he had tried to do was for Francis. He had never wanted to be a burden on him. Now he wouldn't be.

Merrie, kissed off with merely a mention, was philosophical. After all, Flinty had never been interested in her. Ever a woman of action, she had, as soon as she could, taken a collapsed Frank to that equestrian place in Connecticut where the psychoanalysts and physical therapists had their way with him. He emerged six months later, lacking a certain snap but resigned, as he said, to life, such as it was.

His doctors, in private conversation with Merrie, who was footing the bills, advised her to be careful. Frank Jones was a fragile young man. At the first sign of depression, they were to be consulted. Like a car with defective turn signals, Frank said, having heard this: not real trouble but potentially dangerous.

Merrie had, she said, raised her antennae after Myra's death. Myra had been the only nurturing adult woman in Frank's youth and she had cared for him in a way she had never cared for her own son. It wouldn't be too much to say Frank felt as if he had lost a mother. But other than his usual mood swings, Frank had seemed appropriately sad after Myra's death and nothing more. True, he had been more silent than usual but he was, after all, in mourning.

On this Monday morning, Frank didn't go into the tin shack, his old home. He never did; the wood beam was still there. Instead, he wandered about the junkyard, cruising up and down the dirt byways, discovering old friends among the detritus: the airplane propeller and the Studebaker engine hood and the wooden-wheeled bicycle and the pink and white Versailles-inspired doghouse.

Flinty's time capsule, he thought, looking at the mountains of stuff. In a thousand years they'll excavate it and discover everything they need to know about life in a twentieth-century village.

He tripped over a damaged air pump and fell; a shard of glass from a ship's lantern cut through his jodhpurs and wounded his knee. He had trouble staunching the bleeding with his handkerchief and so he sat still, trying to remember from a long-ago science course how long it would take to bleed to death. He thought it was not such a bad out, poetic in its way: dripping off like a reverse IV onto the pebbly ground of his father's junkyard.

Flinty and Myra had both been bled to death, he thought, hearing the distinctive sound of the Roller's horn. Bled by friends and neighbors. He limped toward the gate and the car and Merrie's care.

"Naturally I carry a first aid kit; what could you be thinking of, dearie?" Lying back in the leather passenger seat, submitting to Merrie's hydrogen peroxide and expert bandaging, Frank told her how he had thought he was dying in the junkyard, to which Merrie said, "Pooh. It's barely a scratch."

As Merrie drove to their handsome brick house, so removed from Flinty's tin shack, Frank wondered if he would ever purge himself of the hate he felt.

"What do you think you're doing?"

"I'm putting the top down. What does it look like I'm doing?"

"You're mad. My hair. I only just had it done . . ."

Mike Bell completed the process of putting the top down. "Personally, I like it better when your hair isn't cemented into place. You look more like a human being."

Lettie, feeling like Alexandra Del Lago in *Sweet Bird of Youth*, said to her own Chance Wayne, "It's your tact that I am so utterly enthralled with, Michael."

"No, it's not," he said, taking her hand and placing it on the part of his person he held sacred. "Can't you call me Mike, like everyone else? You sound like my third-grade teacher."

"I never did go in for diminutives," a wretched Lettie said, not retracting her hand, saying a quick silent prayer to whomever or whatever was up there to wake her from this nightmare, vowing that this was the last time, in life or on stage, when she was going to play the pathetic older woman. The humiliation was intense but then so was the ecstasy.

"No," Mike said, manipulating her hand. "I know you are one lady who does not go in for diminutives."

"I have a question," Lettie announced, finally getting her hand back, seeing that the UPS person in the van next to them was fascinated from above by the action.

"Shoot."

"Why do you invariably take this roundabout back from Southampton and why do you insist on driving through Duck Farm Acres and why, when you do, do you become so especially difficult? Is it some maudlin need to grovel in what-might-have-been?"

"Shut up, Lettie." He stopped the full-sized vintage black-and-white Mercedes ragtop in the center of the horseshoe of expensive, not very adventurous but ambitiously landscaped houses. Most were empty, waiting for summer occupants. Their oversized windows looked out on the picturesque and much photographed pond designed—this was made much of in the prospectus—by a well-known pond architect.

"The pond's about ten times as big as it was when we owned the place," Mike Bell said. "The damn developer knew what he was doing. Made a fortune. Everyone did but us. Jesus, we didn't know diddly-squat."

"I love that expression, diddly-squat," Lettie said, fingering the mother-of-pearl buttons on her suit jacket. She wasn't all that sympathetic to Mike Bell's vision of a lost fortune. The Bells had been so very stupid about their real estate. Waterfront real estate, yet. They had owned these fifty or so acres from the time it was a hardscrabble duck farm to the moment when raising ducks was declared unhealthy and illegal in the township of Southampton. Not knowing what else to do, they sold it for peanuts.

And then the zoning board council agreed—this had, of course, already been set up by the principal investors—that though the land wasn't legal for duck breeding, it was well nigh perfect for residential development.

Then the new developers—poor Myra and Flinty Jones—had lost their shirts and the real powers strolled in, picked up the pieces, and made a fortune. Hard cheese on Myra and Flinty. Hard cheese on the Bells.

But looked at another way, it might have been a stroke of luck for the Bells. Had they been a touch more energetic, they would have borrowed money from the bank and erected an eyesore of a motel called the Dew Drop Inn and lost everything anyway. Visionaries, Lettie thought, the Bells were not.

"Fuckin' rich people just get richer," Mike said, reiterating his father's not so very original thought. Driving the car out of Duck Farm Acres, he headed for Waggs Neck via rural roads at his usual breakneck speed. Lettie reached for his arm but he shook her hand off. His cheap, handsome, brutal face had shut down like a dis-reputable bar at closing time.

"Anyone ever tell you you're the spitting image of John Dillinger?"

"Who the fuck is John Dillinger?" he asked without wanting to know. So many of Lettie's allusions were Greek to him.

Lettie, feeling a not-to-be-denied thrill of anticipation in her nether regions, happily suspected their matinee was going to be more punishing than usual.

"Hey."

"What do you want?"

"Come on, Cora. Like I'm here to apologize."

"Apology not accepted. Could you take it somewhere else? I got like work to do."

"Maybe we should talk about work. I need some background stuff."

"Fine," Cora said, whirling around in her revolving office chair, nostrils flaring. "Fine. You go through channels, Detective Pasko. Like everyone else. Talk to your boss, get him to sign a three-oh-three-one-A, and then have him send it to my boss and if my boss okays it, then his secretary will put it in that stack of maybe two hundred requests for information and I'll get to it long about September of 2001. Unless it gets lost and then we have to start all over again. Keep your big fat paws off me."

"I'm like really sorry, Cora."

"Ditto. Get out."

He shut the door behind him with his foot and knelt down beside her, looking up into her tough, cute face. "I get hard whenever I think of you, baby."

"You and your hand could have a lovely relationship."

"I don't believe in marriage, Cora, what can I tell you?"

"Keep off me and stand up. Suppose somebody walked in?"

This was said in a less strident voice.

"Give me a kiss." His hands with their not scrupulously clean fingernails were moving their way up her legs.

"Fuck you," Cora said without much gusto.

"That's just what I want, honey," Pasko whispered in his special husky voice that made her insides feel like jelly.

"What do you think you're doing?" Cora asked, whispering back, making a mild attempt to keep his hands from going up her skirt. "Anybody could come in at any minute . . ."

"I'll cut it out if you promise you'll eat with me tonight. That's all I'm asking. No fooling around. Just dinner. I'll be at your place at six and we'll order in. Deal?"

"If that's the only way I can get you to stop," Cora said, knowing there were any number of ways to get him to stop. "And I'm not pulling up any of your lousy background material, either," she called after him, scanning the list he left on her desk, smoothing her skirt. "You go through channels."

Early the next morning Cora was at her already dated new IBM, once again cross-indexing the names of five women, the first four of them dead.

Chapter
14

"SHIT. HERE COMES THE PUD OF ALL PUDS TO MAKE MY DAY,"
Yolanda said, loud enough for Wyn to hear but low
enough for Wyn to ignore, which she did.

"They're in there?" Wyn asked, pointing to the door
that led to Homer's office.

"Jez," Yolanda acknowledged, speaking loudly to
compensate for the hearing loss caused by the reggae
beat of the music playing in the Sony portable head-
phones inserted in her pretty, mega-pierced seashell
ears.

"Would you like to announce me?" Wyn asked
with patience.

"Uh-uh. They're waiting for you." Yolanda wasn't
sure why but, as she told her best friend, "I just get
myself off on dissing that bitch. I can not help myself.
It's that wrong way of dressing and that right way of
talking and that *Vogue* face and . . ." Yolanda could
and did go on about the many ways Wyn irritated her.

Wyn started toward the door but then decided that allowing Yolanda to get away with sassiness once would mean letting her get away with it forever. "You like your job, Yolanda?" she pivoted and asked. Not surprisingly, the words came out in her mother's high school principal voice, heavy on the diction.

Yolanda didn't know where this was going but she was game. "So so."

"Well, if you don't get a civil tongue in your dye-damaged head, Yolanda, I'm going to propose half a dozen people to take your place, any one of whom could do it better, nicer, and maybe even less expensively than you. Here's the moral of this story: You talk to me in an appropriate way when you talk to me at all."

Yolanda couldn't resist rolling her huge eyes.

"You do understand what I'm saying?" Wyn asked as if she were talking to a severely impaired person. And who knew?

"Yes, ma'am," finally came out of Yolanda's ripe, magenta-red lips as she forced herself to sit still and not slap that angelic and, all right, beautiful face.

"Great," Wyn said, wondering why she so often felt she had to be the enlightener, the Miss Manners of Waggs Neck Harbor. Wyn was a bit ashamed. Yolanda, though she started it, was, after all, easy pickings. She wondered if she shouldn't kill a lunch hour and have a heart-to-heart with Yolanda as she headed for the meeting from hell.

It didn't disappoint. The atmosphere was so gelatinous with distrust and dismay you could cut it with a plastic knife. "What's a pud?" Wyn asked, hoping to defuse some of this electricity.

"A fat, stumpy dick, the kind that can't get hard." Pasko was sitting in the oak visitor's chair. He was wearing his other gabardine suit—this one brown and short in the leg, revealing white athletic socks and standard-issue black lace-ups.

The latter was the only thing he had in common with Homer, who sat behind his desk, looking as starched as his uniform and about as yielding as the African god Lucy Littlefield swore he resembled and yearned to worship.

"Have you ever thought of replacing Yolanda?" Wyn asked Homer, ignoring Pasko's information and her own good resolves to make peace with Homer's secretary.

"You tell me how to get rid of Yolanda, who knows more about civil service rights and benefits than the three of us put together, and I'll buy you a chicken dinner every Sunday for the rest of your life."

"You two think we could maybe get down to like business?" Pasko asked.

"What is the business?" Wyn asked from the depth of the oversized second visitor's chair.

"You. Captain Midnight—beg pardon—Captain Price and I have different theories about the murderer but we're pretty much in agreement about the next murderee."

"And who might that be?" Wyn asked, not liking the bubbles suddenly churning around in her tummy. Someone who might know was about to give voice to her private fear. She did not want to hear it.

"You, Wyn," Homer said softly.

There was a moment of quiet. "Sez who?" Wyn asked, belligerently, breaking it.

"Sez the computer," Pasko said. "I had all the statistics run through over the weekend and here's what they came up with: You, and you alone, share a number of key characteristics with the other victims. You're female. You're a successful Realtor. You're a descendant of one of the old East End land-owning families. You were a partner in a shitload of deals with Kathleen C. and Mrs. St. Cloud, deals that pissed off a lot of people.

"Not only that," he went on, holding up his hand to forestall Wyn. "You worked with both female victims from what I believe was the first round of murders. Cross-indexing the transactions McFee and Leverage worked on with the real estate deals St. Cloud and Carruthers were mixed up in all led to a single transaction—the duck farm scam—and one single name: Wynsome Lewis. You're the only one of those women involved in the duck farm who's still walking, talking, and breathing."

Wyn, who wished she smoked so she could do something with her hands, settled on gripping the arms of her seat, which made her feel as if she were strapped into an economy electric chair. "And who," she asked Homer, "if you believe this nonsense, is the person out to get me?"

"A lot of people got shafted during the duck farm's rehabilitation into a fancy community," Pasko answered. "I think we're going to find the killer among them. So does the captain," Pasko said, standing up, hitching up his short, tight trousers, feeling an itch, wondering if Cora had given him crabs.

"But like here's where we differ. I think the killer is the nutsky that offed McPhee and Leverage ten years ago and has been steaming ever since. Now he's erupting, finishing the job.

"Your captain thinks this has got nothing to do with the McPhee-Leverage killings."

"I'm only saying," Homer said tightly, "that maybe there's no connection. Maybe this killer is using the earlier murderer's MO to mislead us. Maybe it's a coincidence. Maybe you got a fixation."

"Yeah. Like navy-blue panty hose are every revenge freak's favorite weapon."

"Panty hose," Homer returned, "have been the strangler's weapon of choice since the Boston Strangler popularized them. Have your crime techs found out if they're all the same brand, bought at the same time?"

"If you read the report I faxed you . . ."

". . . and I never received . . ."

". . . the earlier ones were purchased at the Bridgehampton IGA in September of 1985. The new ones were bought at the Bridgehampton Caldors a few weeks ago. Different manufacturers: the first were made by the Japs, the new ones are from Taiwan. None of it proves nothing. I know, way deep down in my nuts, that this is the same perp.

"Listen, Captain Mid— Captain Price. How's this for a game plan? You get busy on your no-connection theory; knock yourself out. Meanwhile, I'll work on my serial killer. We'll talk every day and pool our findings. If one of us seems to be getting anyplace, we concentrate on that. This should keep my boss and the senator happy. Okay by you?"

Homer admitted it was okay by him.

"And what about me?" Wyn asked as Pasko made departure movements, not caring much whether it was a new killer or an old killer but caring that there was a chance it was *her* killer.

"You? We spent the time while we were waiting for you, Ms. Handwerk, figuring out what you should be doing. Captain Midnight here is going to fill you in."

"Probably be most efficient if I let myself be strangled," Wyn said. Panic seemed to be creeping in on big feet in Corfam shoes.

"You got that right," Pasko agreed. "But we want to keep you alive."

"Why?"

"I don't know about the captain but the truth is I'm hoping that you'll be so goddamned grateful, you'll hop into bed with me."

He was halfway out the door when he heard Wyn call after him, "You pud."

"Not really." He closed the door behind him, smiled at the Technicolor sight of Yolanda's head and the memory of Wyn's feistiness, and headed out for Montauk to have a talk with the late Kathy Carruthers's secretary.

"Homer, can we go somewhere else to have this discussion? Maybe over lunch. Fear and anguish always make me hungry. Your office is nice and neat but after the sewer rat Pasko contaminated it, I need a change of venue. Some place safe. Tell me someone's not going to try to strangle me. Please."

She was disappointed when her hard-won friend, Homer Price, didn't make soothing, don't-be-stupid noises.

Chapter
15

THEY FOUND A HAVEN AT A TABLE IN THE DARKEST CORNER of the womblike La Salle à Manger, the exclusive "waiter-service only" section of La Pizzeria. Homer had allowed that it would be okay if Tommy joined them.

Tommy, who had been working in East Hampton, made it in record time. He hadn't liked the sound of Wyn's voice when she asked him if he wanted to have lunch. She never had time for lunch with him. He found her scarfing down thick slices of flaming hot Sicilian All-the-Way. "Are you crying?" he asked Wyn, immediately and totally concerned.

"It's the red pepper I put on," she managed to say, reaching for her diet Coke.

Homer, a man Tommy admired for his restraint, was carefully carving a thin slice of the house pizza with fork and knife, looking at Wyn with controlled disgust, as if he were her nanny. "I'm not good with pizza,"

Wyn admitted, strands of melting extra extra cheese connecting her fingers to her mouth.

Tommy sat down, looking askance at the straw-wrapped Chianti bottles perched tentatively on a ledge above him. Green plastic ivy crawled up the lattice walls trying for a cottage effect. Color-coordinated bug repellent candles stood on each plastic-covered table emitting a chemical odor. A pair of louvered saloon doors connected La Salle à Manger to the more plebeian, serve-yourself section in the front.

When the waiter, a Pizza family member named Wayne, ambled over, asking if Tommy wanted to see the menu, Tommy said no, he wanted a dish of spaghetti, al dente, with plain tomato sauce. Nothing to drink. Just a glass of water.

"A glass of water is something to drink," Wayne instructed.

"You still not eating meat?" Homer wanted to know, blotting his lips with a paper napkin.

"I try not to eat anything with eyes," Tommy admitted.

"Potatoes?"

"Potatoes are cool as long as you avoid the skin and don't overdo it. Member of the deadly nightshade family."

"Guys, do you think we could get off weird eating habits and on to the subject at hand?"

"What's that?" Tommy asked, smelling his spaghetti, which had arrived with suspicious speed. "I told you, Wayne, I wanted it al dente."

"Get real, Tommy. We make all our spaghetti in the morning. That's as al dente as you're going to get."

"Tommy," Wyn said as Wayne went back to his beer in the kitchen, "Homer and that *vantz*, Detective Pasko . . ."

"What's a *vantz?*" Homer wanted to know.

"It's Yiddish for bedbug," Tommy explained, having picked up a number of such phrases in the year he had been married to Wyn, who in turn had picked them up from her first husband.

"Do you two mind if I finish a sentence? Homer and Pasko believe that I'm the next victim. Worse, I believe I'm the next victim."

"What?"

Homer explained, gently, how his thought processes and Pasko's computers and Wyn's gut feelings all led to the possibility that the killer was going to try to strangle Wyn.

"I guess you could dig it," Tommy said evenly after Homer finished. Pragmatism was a stratagem he retreated to when faced with unwanted news: After his mother had been nearly blown away by a reckless driver, his first reaction had been that she was always careless in traffic.

Returning his attention to his spaghetti, Tommy went on in his deliberate, nonemotional tone: "I mean a whole bunch of families in the village have had it stuck to them by the Realtors. My own mom . . ."

Wyn considered punching him in his flawless nose but decided to keep it verbal. "If you tell that story about that broken-down shanty by the old railroad track one more time, Handwerk, I'm going to run out into the street and scream. But why bother with my old crimes? There's surely enough contemporary evidence to convict right now. Maybe we should have a public execution," Wyn went on, loudly.

Tommy put his big, delicious, wood-smelling hand over her sauce-smeared mouth and said, "I am sorry. I am very sorry. I don't know how to deal with this. But it ain't easy believing someone wants to kill you, of all

David A. Kaufelt

people." The reversion to the old telltale "ain't" gave away the fact that Tommy was having real trouble.

Not one for letting anyone, especially Tommy, off easy, Wyn went on, "There's all the elderly widows and blind orphans that I cheated, selling their lame cottages to unsuspecting aliens when they were really teardowns . . ."

Tommy tried to interrupt but Wyn was on a roll. "And then there's all the deadly nightshade potato farmers who thought they could do it themselves and linoleumed and bideted and plastic chandeliered and in general messed up forever their plain Jane barns which sat empty until I was able to sell them to a New Yorker who had to undo everything they did before starting from scratch."

"Wyn . . ."

"Oh, I know, you handy East Enders and your facility for woodworking and home-assembled wind chimes and granny's macramé plant holders. But none of you seem to have the touch needed to turn termite-eaten dross into chintz-upholstered gold. Shall we talk about your Uncle Thurmond's log cabin effort, Tommy?" Whereupon Wyn put her head down on the vinyl tablecloth and began to cry.

Tommy buried his face in her hair and Homer said he had to, ahem, use the facilities.

"You're scared," Tommy said, after Wyn had recovered a bit.

"You bet I'm scared. I don't want to walk into an empty house and come out feet first, my neck decorated in the new panty hose style. Hold me."

He did so, saying he was scared, too, but if she took precautions . . .

"Oh, Homer has a whole list of wise precautions. That's the reason behind this dumb lunch. He and that

114

low-life Pasko are having the time of their lives running around playing detective while I'm supposed to be busy taking wise precautions."

Homer emerged from the men's room, saw that Wyn was sitting up, dry-eyed, and resumed his seat to regale her and Tommy with more wise precautions.

The most important of these was that Wyn was not to show any properties without first thoroughly vetting the potential client. She was not to proceed with the showing unless the recently promoted Sergeant Ray Cardinal, always on call via mobile phone, was alerted and agreed to accompany or meet her at the property. If Ray was otherwise occupied, the captain himself would be available. If he couldn't make it, Tommy or any able-bodied person would be an appropriate escort.

"Bottom line, Wyn: You are not to go on any showings without your cellular phone switched on and without someone moderately big and strong going with you."

"How about Liz Lum?" Wyn wanted to know.

"Only if the client is a blind, one-armed, clubfooted octogenarian in a wheelchair," Homer said with rare sarcasm. "Use your common sense, Wyn."

"Homer," Wyn said, judiciously dividing the check three ways, adding on a grudging twelve point five percent for Wayne's gratuity, "why aren't you more nervous? One of your very best friends, a woman who has gone through thick and thick with you, has her life threatened. Don't you think it would be appropriate if you . . ."

". . . Wyn . . ."

". . . evinced some emotion like . . ."

"Shut up, Wyn." Homer had only asked her to shut up once before and she knew having to say it stretched his politeness parameters to the max. "I think I know who did it."

"Who?"

"Too early to say but I doubt if you're going to allow yourself to be in an empty house with him."

"He may not be confined to one modus operandi," Wyn said, leading the way out of the dining room, half convinced by the conviction in Homer's sincere basso profundo voice.

"I thought," Tommy objected, "it was supposed to be a woman who called Petro and Kathy Carruthers?"

"Murderers have been known to have accomplices," Homer said instructively, not admitting that was one of the holes in his theory. This kind of murderer rarely needed help.

Chapter

16

ON TUESDAY MORNING WAGGS NECK HARBOR POLICE CHIEF Homer Price, starched and resolute, marched across Main Street to the New Federal to interview the hotel's food and beverage manager, Michael Bell.

He ostentatiously used the pedestrian zone though there wasn't a car in sight. Despite Homer's fine example, swarms of citizens were crossing Main Street wherever they damn well felt they could.

"You want to arrest me, Captain, be my guest." A pink-garbed Lucy Littlefield was deliberately jaywalking, pushing her grandnephew in his elaborate stroller across the street. "And arrest this child whilst you're at it. Arrest the whole damn town if you got a mind to. We're all victims of the fascist government in this village, as if you didn't know."

Homer, thinking Lucy Littlefield was arrested enough, ignored her and concentrated on his forthcoming interview. He was hip to the fact that he was going to have to squeeze every last drop out of his self-control tube to be fair and square with Mike Bell.

It wasn't only Mike. It was all the Bells who rang his chimes, swarming around Waggs Neck Harbor like the rats of Hamelin, getting into all kinds of heavy mischief.

Precisely because he longed to chop them up and feed them to the fish, Homer was extra careful to treat them with scrupulous courtesy, with unfailing if remote respect. They, in turn, complained that Captain Midnight singled them out for every infraction; that he had it in for them.

He regretted that he had been so definite in telling Wyn and Tommy that he knew who the murderer was. But she had seemed relieved and Homer had felt somewhat confident. Not that he had much proof. Mike Bell was his candidate for several solid reasons but also because Mike didn't have a grain of compassion in his beefy being. He told himself that he would start slowly with the incendiary Mike. If Mike did do it, Homer didn't want to muddy the prosecution's case with claims of police brutality. All Homer wanted to find out, for the moment, was where Mike had been when Petronella St. Cloud and Kathy Carruthers were killed.

A belated flash sent on from the West Sea medical examiner's office via Pasko stated that Kathy Carruthers had been strangled late on Friday afternoon, not on Saturday morning, as had been supposed.

It would have been a snap—Homer regretted the phrasing—for Mike Bell, with his hard-earned bench-press muscles, to have killed the two women. "Like strangling not only takes balls, Captain, you got to have muscle, too," Pasko had informed him patronizingly.

Homer turned his thoughts back to Mike Bell. He

had a nice motive. He was the least forgiving of the Bells, most of whom took their lumps with a lot of noise and quickly got over them with breezy nonchalance.

And, contrary to popular opinion, Homer believed Mike had the brains for it. Both occasions had called for a more than average intelligence. Leaving behind no prints, no fibers, no personal liquid or hair strands or bits of skin—no sign of human presence whatsoever—took either supernatural power or some intricate thought.

What's more, in order to leave behind such a clean crime scene, the killer had to be highly organized. He had had to know what to bring and what to leave at home. He had to be comfortable, as Pasko pointed out, with this kind of crime; he probably had to have done it before.

Ten years ago, when McFee and Leverage were killed, Mike Bell had been barely out of his teens but even then he had possessed those off-putting wiles that led Homer to believe he was up to most any kind of deception. It looked as if—Jesus, how Homer didn't like admitting this—Pasko was right and one person had killed all four women. But the question remained: Why would the killer (Mike Bell?) wait a decade between killings? New information as to Petronella's and Kathy's involvement in the duck farm scam might have done it, but there had been plenty of incriminating evidence from the top.

Homer was distracted from these thoughts as a few drops hit the visor of his cherished chief's hat. He looked up, checking to make sure it was rain and not an importunate bird. Clouds were speeding in from the bay signifying an April shower.

He stepped into the New Federal's grandiose vision

of a Victorian lobby just as the rain came down in ear-
nest. The room was empty except for a group of heavily
wattled ladies having tea around one of a set of six
carved, white wood elephant tables. These were used
during the summer season by self-conscious literati in
Tom Wolfe suits playing low stakes backgammon and
by important artists' widows holding court in elaborate,
avoirdupois-camouflaging caftans.

On more than one occasion there had been an un-
seemly scuffle for the tables, resulting in hard words
and sore bottoms—as in the case when a *Newsday* reporter kicked a *New York Times* columnist where he said
it would do the most good. Lettie had finally installed
a reservations book, which only created a new competition: who could get their names in first.

Restrained nods were exchanged between Homer and
the tea-takers who followed his progress across the yel-
low-and-blue faux-Chinese carpet to where that little
tart Victoria Bell was standing behind the ebony-and-
glass front desk.

"Hey, Victoria. Your brother Mike around?" The languid and eerily beautiful Bell child-woman smiled. She
was studying the complex designs on her painted, arti-
ficial fingernails as if they contained the revelations for
which the world was waiting. She wore a dress that, in
the proper light, revealed all of New York.

"Maybe he's at the Spa. Got to work two jobs, Mike
does. Owes money all over the place. Or maybe he
went home to eat. I could call for you . . ." Or do
anything else you wanted was implied by the way she
put elbows on the counter and looked up into Homer's
innocent Smokey Bear eyes.

Homer said he'd be grateful if she called. He waited,
concentrating on the long mahogany bar's spiffy brass
fittings, thinking real Victorian hotel lobby bars proba-

bly never looked as good as this. He was trying not to take note of the provocative postures in which Victoria was arranging her body; though on Judgment Day he would have to admit that much like one of his presidential heroes, he was lusting in his heart.

"Phone's off the hook," she eventually reported. "And he's not at the Spa. Patty Batista was pissed that I even asked. Like she was surprised I didn't know his schedule. How the hell would I know Mike's schedule?"

Victoria smiled generously at him, clasping her hands in front of her in such a way that her breasts were pushed up and out. Homer suspected that by summer, when the rich, proper writers returned, Victoria would be demoted back to upstairs maid and Lettie would have to spring for a less benevolent front-desk person.

He nodded good-bye to the tea-takers and stepped out into the rain. A number of women and an occasional male were cruising Main Street, attending to morning errands. They looked like extras in an early German sci-fi film in their rainproof "bubble suits," a tried-and-true moneymaker over the years for the Waggs Neck Harbor five-and-dime.

Made of thick, impenetrable plastic, the bubble suits consisted of a colorless visored balaclava helmet with tiny perforations in the nostril vicinity for breathing; a long pullover smock, gathered at the waist and neck; gloves, reminiscent of operating rooms, gathered at the wrists; shapeless trousers gathered about the ankles; and booties that slid over one's shoes and once fastened with snaps but were now new and improved, held together with strips of Velcro. The bubble suits were considered "low" by the middle haute monde, but at ten dollars and ninety-five cents they maintained their popularity among locals and tourists, nevertheless. Homer thought he'd rather just get wet.

*　　*　　*

Homer drove the squad car over Shark Channel Bridge out to the post-World War II subdivision known as Red Wood Shores by its denizens and Red Neck Shores by the residents of the village proper.

A mostly summer and weekend community populated by retired blue-collar workers and service veterans, it appeared to be the one place in the area where spring hadn't yet happened.

Leaf-bare brownish-green third-growth trees and maroon and baby-blue vinyl-coated houses with built-to-last wooden decks vied for plainness with the stolid brown birds waiting for the millennium on the telephone wires.

Homer parked his showroom-condition patrol car in the Bells' half-circular driveway, which was being taken over by a weed garden that possessed a near Asian sense of balance. The neighbors, attempting *House & Garden* gentility, did not subscribe to this Nature as Art practice of nongardening. Whenever the offending weeds grew to the three-foot limit, village law enforcers were called upon to serve summonses, threaten fines, and eventually have the village Department of Roads mow down the weeds and send much contested, never-to-be-paid bills to the Bells.

Randomly strewn within and around the weeds was the largest and most colorful collection of children's toy furniture, play houses, trikes, and trucks this side of the showrooms of Toys "Я" Us. The primary plastic colors, so at odds with the dreary landscape, fairly screamed out to the rare casual passerby with look-at-me-ness.

These playthings belonged to the many grandchildren who often found themselves at the senior Bells' residence thanks to trial separations, bitter divorces,

Fort Lauderdale winter vacations, and Smithtown Mall shopping expeditions.

Homer suspected that not unlike Flinty Jones's junkyard, one day the Bell gardens would be enshrined as one of the last and most durable collections of late-twentieth-century split-level artifacts. His own garden was a masterpiece of manicured lawn surrounding a reconstituted stone wishing well. His children's toys were kept in the playroom where he never had to see them. Homer firmly believed that a messy atmosphere made for a messy life.

The Bell homestead was a nice example. Homer made his way up the cracked concrete path, gingerly stepped on the most secure of the wooden front steps, and knocked on the rotting door. Victor Bell, one of the early foes of employing a black chief of village police, eventually appeared.

Victor looked as shiftless as ever in his Blue Buoy Bar & Grill T-shirt, which had been stretched tautly over his magnificent belly, the ragged sleeves riding up his flabby arms.

"He ain't here," Victor said in a tone that lacked his usual heat. He was remembering the last time Homer came calling, looking for one of his sons. Victor, a master of self-deceit, was unable to avoid reflecting that if he had told Captain Midnight what he had wanted to know then, his son Billy might still be alive. Not that Billy had been any prize, but his mother had loved him. "Victoria called and said you were looking for Mike. Haven't seen him in weeks. Between real estate school and two jobs, that kid doesn't have time for a whizz."

"You think you and I could have a talk?" Homer asked, wondering if the step he stood on was going to hold him; wondering, too, where this sudden shot of pity was coming from. Victor Bell was slime, murdered son or not.

"I ain't got nothing to talk to you about, Captain Midnight." Victor had returned to his old hostility. He let out a belch accompanied by a blast of bad breath, nearly solid in its potency. Sausage, pickles, and beer for late breakfast, Homer decided.

"For Christ sake, let the bastard in. What games are you playing now, Victor? We got nothing to hide . . . that I know about."

This was the shrill, Irish-inflected voice of Mrs. Bell— Teresa—who had emerged from the hell of her eldest and favorite son's murder with a new steely will. Once a shrinking violet, she was now a meat-eating plant.

"I used to want everyone to like me," she had recently confided to Wyn Lewis over green tomatoes at the IGA. "Now I don't give a hot shit."

She was short and growing shorter, a living example of the ravages of calcium deficiency and giving birth to too many Bells; it was as if each of her children had taken a piece of her. Bone thin, she sported gold-framed aviator glasses, the blue-tinted lenses surpassingly thick. Her sparse, recently shampooed brown hair was tucked up on top of her head and held in place with one of her baby granddaughter's red plastic barrettes.

Homer thought her singularly blunt but not unsympathetic. "Something to drink? Pop? Water?" she asked and Homer said no thank you, knowing Victor would feel compelled to break the glass after he left.

"Sit down," she ordered. Homer looked around the narrow, low-ceilinged, desolate living room and settled on a hefty armchair with a stripe-patterned slipcover. Considering the outside confusion, the room was surprisingly neat. "The grandkids and Victor are kept down in the rec room," Teresa said, reading his mind. "This is my space."

Victor stood in the doorway, looking like a whipped dog waiting further humiliation. "You go down and see to Jamie and Pammie," his wife obliged. "I'll take care of Captain Midnight."

Relieved, Victor disappeared and Teresa Bell and Homer Price looked at one another, seriously. Admittedly, there was no love lost between the two of them but their disaffection did not preclude respect.

"What is it this time? Or who is it this time? Speak up and let's get this over with. I ain't going to withhold, Captain. I learned once what 'protecting' my kids can do to them. Which one is it? Ding Dong? Ralphie? Drugs? Stealing?" An unthinkable thought came to her. "No one's hurt, are they?" The specter of her dead son made itself felt. It had been Homer who had had to tell her.

"No one's hurt, Mrs. Bell. No one's even in trouble, yet. I just need a little history."

"About what?"

"The duck farm."

"Why?" Teresa Bell saw the way Homer looked at her and knew she wasn't going to get an answer and decided she could live with that. Had Victor told him what he wanted to know three years ago, Billy might still be alive. I might still be alive, she thought.

Teresa knew she couldn't think about Billy. When she did, she wept and she sure didn't want to bawl in front of Midnight. So she lit a Marlboro, found a glass ashtray Victoria had liberated from the New Federal, and told him about the duck farm.

"Before Victor, I was a Crossmeyer, you know." This announcement was accompanied by a slight lift of her narrow chin and for a moment Homer saw how handsome she had once been and where the Bell progeny got their looks.

"By the time I came along we were poor but not trash: we still owned the duck farm. The smell alone could kill you. But it was ours and we made a living out of it until Father passed away and Mother let it out to her no-account brother. Then she passed on and I ended up married to Victor Bell and Jesus wept.

"That no-account vanished one night owing us a year's rent and stripping the farm of everything but the ducks. Then the county zoning board up and outlawed duck breeding; said it was unhealthy.

"Not one damn soul had gotten sick from those ducks in over thirty years but suddenly they were the Typhoid Marys of poultry. This was back in 1985. We were getting set to lose the whole kit and caboodle to taxes when Petronella St. Cloud came along with an offer that wasn't so hot but we didn't see how we could refuse it.

"There was no mortgage but there was the taxes and we were broke. Nor was our gang capable of cleaning up the place or getting the permits and all that hooey to try to turn it into something the zoning board would approve for housing.

"I didn't much trust Petronella. And she was working with Kathy Carruthers, a lady I never had any faith in. So we got Wyn Lewis, just back in town, to represent us. We knew her dad and we thought she'd be fair. We walked away with maybe ten thousand dollars plus change."

Homer knew the rest but Teresa was into it and he let her go on, telling him how the new owners had such big plans. Myra Fiske Stein and Flinty Jones, of all people. They leveled the rickety duck farm buildings, carted away the accumulated duck effluvium, cleaned up the pond, and only then found out the banks weren't going to give them any more money. The banks didn't believe in them; or the banks were told not to believe in them.

"Myra Fiske Stein, the Princess of Waggs Neck Harbor, ended up a bankrupt and she took Flinty Jones under with her. Then the so-called consortium brats came in, bought the property, and made millions developing it."

"That must have felt real good," Homer said, sympathetically.

"You don't have enough imagination to understand how we felt. Ripped off by Myra, ripped off mostly by the damned Realtors whose advice we were dumb enough to take. The entire deal was set up from the beginning. Who do you think sat on the zoning board and who do you think minted money every time the property turned over? Petronella St. Cloud, may she rot in hell.

"Not to mention Kathy Carruthers and your buddy, Wyn Lewis. Every time they turned the property, they made more money." She checked each incident off, striking her right thumb against her left fingers beginning with her sad pinky. "First when they got us to sell it to Myra Fiske Stein and Flinty. Second, when they got the consortium to buy it from the banks. And third and fourth and fifth, every time they sold one of the condos to the New Yorkers for a million bucks. Your so-called real estate ladies," Teresa ended up, looking as if she were going to spit on the shag carpet.

"Victor got good and drunk for the next year," she went on, her mouth twisted in disgust. "But most of the kids didn't care, having other twaddle on what passes for their minds. I don't know why folks have children. Pigs is what they ought to have. At least you can eat pigs.

"Anyway, it was Mike who took it really bad. He even talked to our cousin's husband over in Patchogue, a lawyer. The lawyer said the whole thing stunk to high heaven but the truth was that we needed a lot of money to just start suing and even then, with the people involved, we didn't have a prayer. We were lucky we got our ten grand.

"This made Mike even crazier. He was famous for having the sulks as a kid but since the duck farm business, he's always at the short end of his fuse. He used to have a little common sense; now it's all gone. He just made the mistake of borrowing money from a down-island Shylock to buy himself that Mustang convertible. He's having trouble meeting the vigorish the bastard is charging. The poor kid's still making payments on the down payment. Or, more likely, Lettie Browne is."

Teresa smiled for the first time ever at Homer but it wasn't a smile brimming over with good cheer. It was the smile of a woman whose life has been a disappointment; the smile of a woman who has nothing to look forward to and nothing in her past to give her comfort.

Homer felt compassion but he knew Teresa didn't want that—or anything—from him. "Any more questions, Midnight?" She looked exhausted.

"You think Mike killed Petronella St. Cloud?" Homer asked, using his last bullet.

"No," Teresa Bell said triumphantly, deflecting it. "When Petronella St. Cloud was getting what she deserved, Mike was in bed with Lettie Browne giving her what she's paying for. And we have a witness."

"Lettie?"

"Besides her. Our Victoria. She's always been a peeper. She was on her knees Saturday morning just at the time the papers say Petro was strangled. She was looking through the keyhole of Mike's room while he was doing what he does best to Lettie Browne."

For a New York minute Homer wondered if Teresa wasn't a potential murderer. She had the cunning and the time and the venom but as she stood up, using the chair arm to help her, letting her gaze fix on a high school picture of her dead son, he realized she had neither the strength nor the determination. Teresa Bell was still a mother in mourning.

Homer left the Bells' house thinking about Mike Bell's alibi. There was no putting it off: He was going to have to have a talk with Lettie Browne, an eventuality that struck terror in his teeth. There was something unforgiving about Lettie Browne that reduced his considerable presence to near nothingness. He decided, as he picked his way through the Bells' plastic toy garden, that he would get Wyn to do it.

He was aware that he, all by himself, was going to have to tackle those "unnatural children," Frank and Merrie Jones.

Chapter
17

⟨❦⟩

IT WAS COOL AND GRAY, MORE LIKE THE APRIL DAYS WYN remembered from her youth when anything—weather, love, personal and global disaster—was possible. Hitler, she recalled, was born in April.

She was trying to keep her fears under control by concentrating on irrelevancies. This wasn't so easy when, as was so often the case, irrelevancies had that odd way of turning themselves into relevancies.

She had woken too early and had gone into the room she called her office, where she kept her home files and her father's old books, looking for a mystery to read. She wanted the comfort of the known and immediately found what she was looking for in *The Mysterious Affair at Styles.*

She sank down in the old davenport with a great big sigh of happy anticipation and would have started to read if her eye hadn't caught a newspaper clipping tacked to the bulletin board next to her.

It was a year or so old and featured a photo taken of the head table at the annual East End Realtors' Ball. Petronella was in the center, looking especially formidable. Kathy Carruthers was to her right, looking especially frowsy. To Petro's left was Wyn wearing her customary ice cube smile for the camera. The cut line named them, referring to them as the three most important Realtors on the East End, "each of them, when it comes to annual sales, a multimillion-dollar baby." How Petronella must have enjoyed that description. Not.

Even Agatha Christie wasn't going to soothe Wyn after that. The quickly aging photo made all three of them look like resurrected corpses and it didn't take much of Wyn's imagination to see panty hose wrapped around all of their necks.

She pulled the clipping off the bulletin board, balled it up, deposited it in the appropriate receptacle, and decided there was nothing to do but get on with her day.

She completed her limited toilette, which consisted mostly of preventive dentistry: flossing, brushing, Water Piking. Her dentist was a scary man, especially on the topic of the encroaching tooth decay of middle age; photos of otherwise nice-looking folks exposing green stumps and blackened molars littered his office walls.

Drying her hair with a towel—the dryer was on the fritz—Wyn examined herself critically in the oval mirror she had made Tommy bring up from the living room to their bathroom, even though he said it didn't "go." How would he know what went and didn't, that bumpkin?

As she searched for wrinkles, which she found, she wondered if her hair needed just a bit of a cut by whoever was wielding the scissors this month down at Waggs Neck Harbor Coiffeurs.

She emerged from the bathroom, which had once been a fourth bedroom until her father had gotten the idea of creating a second upstairs bath out of plumbing fixtures relegated by ancient Lewises to the basement.

Wyn liked the bathroom, despite its inconveniences. Tommy wanted to "upgrade" it. You want an upgraded bathroom, she had told him, you move to a motel. In time, Tommy had seen the charm of the existing bathroom and focused his creative abilities on transforming the garage into a workshop for himself. The attic, he said, often, would make a great nursery.

"Soon as you start a day-care center," Wyn had told him, but she hadn't liked his nonresponse. "Of course you want a child," she went on. "A spiffy little boy with blond hair and a baseball glove. He'll validate your manhood."

"It just might validate your womanhood, too," Tommy returned, having learned the rudiments of the game.

Wyn knew in her heart that Tommy should have a child, being the kind of good-natured fellow who threw balls for bored dogs and was up on sports. He would make a terrific dad, not unlike her own. My dad, Wyn reflected, should have had a boy. Mother, she thought, should have remained barren.

Wyn had even been lately admitting, if only to herself, that she sort of, kind of wanted a child, but didn't like the thought of having one. Talk of epidurals and Lamaze made her mind go blank with fear and disgust. But: she was (a good) thirty-eight and, as amiable enemies thought right to point out, no spring chicken.

Recent events were making her increasingly aware of her mortality and the thought of leaving Tommy and the world without a tiny Wynsome Lewis running around caused a precipitous regret.

Our issue, Wyn said to herself, almost but not quite convinced, will be a great, eccentric beauty as well as the important novelist literate America has been holding its breath for since Faulkner and Fitzgerald passed on. She will be a better person than I am, immune to junk food and *Reader's Digest,* able to give full vent to her sexual fantasies.

The willing sire of that perfect heiress lay snoozing nicely in their bed, white quilt pulled up to his muscular neck, Probity's head, as usual, on his nicely rounded shoulder, the two of them sharing an antiallergenic pillow.

She kissed him on his forehead, smoothed his corn-blond hair out of his closed American-flag-blue eyes, and regarded him for a moment with depth-defying, inexplicable love and desire. Even though they had had a lalapalooza of a fight the night before.

Past mistress at igniting minor conflagrations and fanning them into four alarmers, Wyn had waited until after dinner to light the match. "Just what did you mean when you strolled in here tonight, Handwerk, and said 'hello' like that?"

Tommy knew from her Bette-Davis-on-a-high-horse delivery what was coming but was powerless to stop it. "If that 'hello' is a sign of how much you care about me, I think this relationship is irreparably spoiled."

Wyn started to get up from the dining table, presumably heading for Reno, but Tommy, knowing he didn't have the words, managed to grab her wrist.

He knew she was worried, scared. He wasn't sure she should be but her feelings were real; that much he had learned in group. He didn't know how to calm her but he did know this was not a night when sex could be a panacea.

Wisely, Tommy led her into the living room to the ancient, oversized green sofa and indulged in a goodly amount of pampering and petting and hugging and Daddy-like kisses. After a time, he said, "Would you like to talk about your feelings?"

"Don't you dare social-work me, Tommy," Wyn warned. But she held on to his hand and kept her luminous head buried in his neck. Not all that adept at saying what she wanted, she knew what it was: twenty-four-hour surveillance, Tommy with her every second, armed to the pecs with Colt .44 and bull whip, his entire being devoted to protecting her.

What she was getting was a good-natured mild disbelief and a daily pal-like caution to take care of herself. Wyn decided this was because deep down in the pit of his huge weeping willow tree of a heart, Tommy believed that Petro and Kathy had only gotten what they had earned.

Charged with this as they walked arm in arm upstairs to the bedroom, Tommy denied everything, saying no one deserved to be killed the way in which they were. "How *did* they deserve to be killed?" Wyn asked. "Quartering?"

Tommy made the mistake of laughing.

"I'm glad I tickled your funny bone, Tommy. When I'm found in a deserted house, dead as your love for me, cut-rate panty hose wrapped around my neck, I hope you have a good many chuckles."

Tommy, warning himself to keep his trap shut, kissed Wyn with serious intent. Sex, he reasoned, might be good for what ailed her now.

Wyn, who hated to admit that even the sight of the curly blond hair on his chiseled forearm aroused her, allowed herself to be seduced; though she couldn't help knowing that, in reality, she had been the seducer. Lusty, angry sex turned out to be a perfectly good antidote for fear. She couldn't remember ever having been so afraid and she was ashamed.

She forced herself to stop gazing at Tommy in the dimness of the following morning, knowing she had to face the day. It was not one she looked forward to since it began with an interview with Lettie, segued into a meeting with Homer and Pasko, and ended with a showing of Shadows, Myra Fiske Stein's old Southampton mansion in which Petronella had been strangled. An unwanted mind-Polaroid of that woman's face, her tiny tongue sticking out of her dried up mouth, was quickly banished, replaced by the corrupt cherub visage of her ex-husband.

Unknown to him, Nick Meyer, Wyn's detested ex-husband, was to be her bodyguard. The fact that he invariably packed "heat"—as he colorfully called his .38—was reassuring but she wouldn't dream of telling him that he was to be her protector. His ego would inflate like a helium-filled balloon and he'd be even less possible than usual.

Nick was to evaluate the late Petro's property as a favor to his mother, who had not trusted Wyn's report. "Yes," that woman had said over the transatlantic telephone highway, "Wyn thinks Shadows might do for a guest house but she would be earning a hefty commission if I bought it, and then one must remember her taste is rather simplistic, *n'est-ce pas?*"

"She married me, Ma," Nick said obligingly, knowing how she enjoyed his playing second banana.

"*Exactement.* Now be a good boy and go look at

Shadows and tell me if you think it will do. Who knows? You may get a rather handsome present."

The present was to be Shadows. Nicky was not unaware that Mommy dearest wanted him and his family right next door all summer and every weekend so she could control his second wife and their uncontrollable children and their lively, attorney-based social life.

Nicky, however, was staying put in the Shelter Island forty-room weekend "cottage" his wife had brought to the marriage, and there it was. Still a bit too close to his control-freak ma but on the water and near enough to Waggs Neck Harbor for him to keep tabs on his fascinating ex-wife, Wynsome Lewis-Handwerk. How she had ever brought herself to marry that all-American *schlemiel* was beyond Nick.

But with his mother's last will and testament looming large in his pension plans, he decided to be persuaded into having a look at Petronella St. Cloud's next-to-last resting place.

"What am I going to wear?" Wyn wondered, deciding on her old standby, the gray flannel jumper. It had several assets. It would give Lettie fodder for her wit; it would help communicate to Pasko the seriousness of her disinterest; it would convince Nick the Rat that she had lost her appeal.

She reached into the drawer of the bird's-eye maple chest in which she had kept her underwear and her secrets since she was a small, mistrusting girl and came up with a pair of ancient navy-blue panty hose. She emitted a high-pitched, bona fide scream.

Tommy sat straight up in bed. "What's up?" he wanted to know, instantly, gratifyingly protective. When Wyn told him *"Nada,"* he looked at her and said what he would have liked to have said the night before if Wyn hadn't been so darn attitudinal.

"I love you, Wyn. I do not think of you as a ruthless Realtor. You like money and you get off on making big-time sales but not at the expense of people. You're like your dad, moral and good and sometimes kind, and I know it's hard for you to say how you feel and ask favors but if you want me to put the East Hampton job on hold and be your bodyguard, the answer is yes and we can start this morning."

"Your client would have your liver served on toast for breakfast, Tommy," Wyn said, tempted to take him up on his offer, but deciding definitely not. He had his career and she had hers and Nick the Rat would be adequate. Probably, no one was out to strangle her and she was wandering adrift in the Paranoid Seas, stirred by Pasko and Homer, making a fool of herself. Looking at the old panty hose lying coiled on the floor, she darned well hoped she was.

She squelched the idea of wearing blusher to offset the gray jumper. No sense in sending mixed messages. "Your client wants to be in that house by Labor Day and she's going to be. But thank you. I don't feel all that threatened this morning. In fact, I think Pasko and Homer are full of horse pucky. The killings are over for at least another decade and we're never going to know why they were committed. If the East End Strangler had wanted to do me in, he's had any number of opportunities. I'm going to be careful but not crazy careful."

She gave him a real kiss, which might have led to more except for the fact that she had seven and a half minutes to meet Lettie for morning coffee; and Tommy's employer was waiting for his arrival to discuss *more* changes to her unfinished East Hampton ocean-front esplanade.

Heading out to meet with Lettie, Wyn put on her brave face, which involved a certain sucking in of cheek and pursing of mouth. She was not going to allow nerves and anxiety to take over. She was not going to let what happened to Petro and Kathy happen to her. She was prepared to use every ounce of her intelligence and ingenuity; she was prepared, she realized with a little shot of pride, to fight back. If necessary.

Chapter

18

THE STEEL AND GLASS BUILDING WAS TOO SQUAT FOR ITS lofty judicial pretensions. The interior—endless tan corridors—produced an existential melancholy that Wyn associated with second-city airports. The West Sea Judicial Complex was probably as good a place to say goodbye as any, she supposed.

Pasko's office was a sparse, government-issue furnished cell; at six feet square, it was still too big for its purpose. A single, inoperable window faced depressing marshlands where the nearly extinct yellow titmouse managed to eke out an existence, despite the warnings of the dedicated wetlands environmentalists who had been bitterly opposed to building on the pristine bayou.

Half a dozen other similar cubicles completed the horseshoe where Pasko and his ilk were stationed. A woman of indeterminate age sat in the center of the horseshoe, simultaneously fielding telephone calls and reading a paperback on self-hypnosis as a cure for problem skin. She told Wyn to go right on in.

Homer—Captain Spit-and-Polish in starched uniform—sat bolt upright in a metal chair a size too small for his bulk.

Pasko was sprawled in a perilously angled desk chair, his Corfams on the gray metal desk, the three top buttons of his shirt undone, revealing a spit curl of black hair.

He was in the position insurance companies and other interested guardians of public safety warn against. Wyn found herself wondering who was going to administer resuscitation if he keeled over backward and split his head open. She'd make Homer do it. It would serve them both right.

"You could put a photograph of your mother on the wall, if only to convince visitors this is a human habitation," Wyn said, sitting in the chair Homer was offering her, asking herself again what it was in Pasko that invariably brought out her acidity.

Not that he wasn't up to it. "Ma's got a harelip, a walleye, and a withered arm. You wouldn't want to see her picture, trust me. What's your pleasure? Weak decaf, warm Coke, stale cheese and peanut butter crackers?"

"Tempting but no thank you. Let's get to it." Wyn decided if she couldn't be civil to Pasko, she could be businesslike. They were meeting in Pasko's office because he said he was sick of commuting to and from Waggs Neck Harbor. The truth was that he liked to give Homer and Wynsome/Losesome a hard time.

"What'd Lettie have to say?" Homer wanted to know, having filled Pasko and Wyn in on Teresa Bell's view of the alleged duck farm scam and his own Mike Bell suspicions.

"She told me my jumper was still darling after all these years. She told me that, sure, she was in bed with Mike Bell on the Saturday morning in question. Seems that's the time he's most aroused; and that, no, she wouldn't swear to Mike's presence unless he was formally charged with Petro's murder. A girl has her reputation, she had the nerve to tell me."

"Where was he on Friday night when Carruthers got chilled?"

"Most of his evening was spent at the college," Homer answered. "He's taking the state real estate salesman's course and he was present and accounted for, and afterwards went for beer with a pair of fellow students.

"This doesn't preclude his killing Kathy Carruthers during the time he left work and showed up for class, but he'd have to drive pretty quick to get out to Montauk and back to fit into the ME's time span. I tried it and it could be done but it was close."

"This is less than an airtight case against Bell," Pasko said, slurping at a dark liquid in a brown mug.

"So who do you like?" Homer asked, wanting to knock Pasko's wide feet off the desk and his curly, cocky head off his broad shoulders.

"I hate to admit it but I'm coming around a bit to your way of thinking, Captain," Pasko said as if he weren't. "I'm still supposing the perp is a Looney Tune and that he's accountable for the earlier icings. But maybe you're right: Our squirrel could be some local who has a real or imagined gripe against your female professionals and every few years he fills his weekend strangling a couple of them."

"Okay. But when you say 'local,' you mean East End or more specific?" Homer asked.

"Maybe more specific."

"Waggs Neck Harbor specific?" Wyn put in.

"Yeah, maybe a Waggs Neck Harbor local." Grilling Pasko was like attempting to open a near-empty childproof bottle. Even when one did, not much came out.

"Care to name a name?" Homer asked, looking at his impressive Timex, standing up, dwarfing the room with his bulk.

"Nope. Not yet. Where you going?"

"I have a meeting with your immediate superior and then, at his request, he and I are interviewing Merrie and Frank Jones."

Pasko was unabashed. "Woo. See if you can find the hair up Captain Savage's ass while you're kissing it. Tons of guys like you have been looking for years."

With palpable self-control Homer moved to the door, gave Wyn his reassuring smile, and said, "Any particular way you want to proceed, Detective?"

"Yeah. After you and the Captain are through jerking off the brother-sister act with warmed kid gloves, I'm going to talk to them myself. The brother looks like he's walking on the thin edge of a razor blade. I want to try to knock him off.

"Meanwhile, Homer, old boy, you might be rethinking the conversation we had while we were waiting for Goldilocks here, and like get back to me. We need a pigeon." Pasko looked at Wyn and smiled.

"Fat chance," Wyn told him, preparing to follow Homer, who was already halfway down the Kafkaesque corridor.

"You sit down," Pasko said to Wyn. "I ain't finished talking to you."

"If you think you're going to set me up as the sacrificial lamb . . ."

"Did I say that? I was talking pigeons. Listen, forget

all that malarkey. Tell me what you know about LeRoy Stein."

Wyn, who had sat down again, said that if Pasko thought that LeRoy Stein . . .

And Pasko said he didn't say he thought that LeRoy Stein did anything, but if she calmed down and listened to what he actually said, all he asked was what did she know about him.

Wyn said she wasn't going to say another word until Pasko told her why he wanted to know. Pasko handed her a Cora-generated computer printout detailing the ins and outs of the various transactions involving the duck farm. It began with the Bells selling it to Myra Fiske Stein and Flinty Jones and ended with the exclusive, highly profitable project put together by Merrie and Frank Jones.

"I still don't . . ."

"If you take a glance at page four, Ms. Handwerk . . ."

"It's Ms. Lewis to you, Pasko. Don't you have a first name? Never mind. I don't want to know." She scanned the page of the report devoted to LeRoy but took a longer time reading the following page, which listed all those who had been involved in bringing about LeRoy's mother's bankruptcy. They included:

Penny McFee and Harriet Leverage, both having prepared legal documents leading to the foreclosure on the hotel.

Petronella St. Cloud, who had profited from Myra's bankruptcy by snapping up Shadows, her Southampton mansion, at a rock-bottom price.

Kathy Carruthers, who, with Wyn Lewis acting as the seller's agent, had been instrumental in getting Myra to buy the duck farm from the Bells.

Frank and Merrie Jones, who bought the duck farm from Myra's creditors for ten cents on the dollar and then had gone about developing Duck Farm Acres and making millions in the process.

"If it were LeRoy," Wyn said, suddenly and thoroughly frightened for her friend, "he should have killed Lettie Browne as well. After all, she ended up with the hotel."

"No, she didn't," Pasko said, sitting up, closing the buttons on his shirt, straightening his knit tie, which had been lying askew on his shoulder like a hangman's noose. "Lettie's brother got the hotel. She only inherited it. And her brother was offed a couple of years ago. Like you don't remember."

"He wasn't strangled, he was poisoned and we know who did it."

"Only hearsay."

"Mine."

"Yeah. LeRoy could have stepped out of his panty hose mode for a second, poisoned Lettie's brother, and *voilà*, one more domino down in his march toward total revenge.

"Plus the fact the dude has no alibis for the times of any of the murders and you can tell the guy's a wacko just by looking at him."

"Have you talked to LeRoy?"

"Yeah, I talked to him. This morning. Sat right in that chair and ran on at the mouth for forty-five minutes and said zilch. The net net of this investigation is that, as the nurse said to the patient while giving him the enema, nothing solid's emerged so far. And like the weekend is coming up. So maybe that's where you come in," Pasko said, moving round the desk, sitting on its rounded corner, hands on knees, expression set on persuasive sincerity.

"Oh, no. This is where I bail. I can't tell you how

charming this has been," Wyn said, refusing to believe that LeRoy could strangle anyone.

"You free tonight?" Pasko asked, getting off the desk.

Standing up and moving away, only to be halted by his incredible *chutzpah,* Wyn asked, "What do you have in mind?"

"Brewskies at my place followed by mud wrestling. Usual Tuesday night routine. What do you say?"

Choosing dignified silence, Wyn retreated out the door as a short, snappy redhead in the discount malls' best strode in. "Who the hell was that?" Wyn heard Cora ask.

"Give me a break, Cora."

"I already gave you one break, Pasko." She kicked the door shut with her four-inch working-girl heels, depriving Wyn and the secretary of hearing more of this entertaining dialogue.

The door flew open almost immediately and Pasko looked out, calling after Wyn, who was at the elevator bank, stabbing at the down button with her index finger. "And don't shoot off your mouth to Baby LeRoy. Our conversation was in confidence."

"Count on it. LeRoy would only laugh in my face." Wyn said this but she wasn't one hundred percent certain it was true. LeRoy was, as the village women had long ago pegged him, one strange duck.

Wyn told herself she didn't believe LeRoy could kill anyone; he was far too polite. Still, she didn't want to run into him any time soon. That choice, however, was not to be left to her.

Chapter
19

Wyn had agreed to nick's request to pick him up at his mother's Southampton beach house out of a not extraordinary motive: self-interest. Nick not only usually carried his revolver, he was a black belt in karate. He had once, single-handedly, made a citizen's arrest of a stout, elderly fellow attempting to steal the tape deck from his Beemer.

Chauffeuring him from one neighboring estate to the other would save her the trouble of getting Homer or Tommy to accompany her to Shadows, a perfect place for Petro's killer to find her.

She drove up the winding, elaborately landscaped driveway and was, as always, amazed at the sheer balls of her ex-mother-in-law's "beach house." To Wyn's jaded silver eyes it resembled Versailles as interpreted by the Fontainebleau Hotel architect with an Olympic-sized pool and a cabana with four bedrooms and baths surrounding a medieval watch tower. It was so grandiose, so ghastly, so architecturally un-p.c., so wrong in the details of its various imitations, it was, well, wonderful.

The housekeeper, who could have stepped into the role of Mrs. Danvers in *Rebecca* with zero rehearsal time, had the fiberglass castle doors open before Wyn could touch the illuminated bell, its surround reputedly made from bits of mosaic stolen from St. Peter's in Rome. "Mr. Meyer said he was tired of waiting."

"I'm five minutes early," Wyn heard herself saying in her rarely used beseeching voice, finding herself once again treated unfairly by her ex-husband, though in the complicated scheme of their various associations, this was a minor and not unpredictable infraction.

They had met when they were students at Brown. Nick had been overly popular, a soccer star, student body pres, a legendary seducer. Though he had attended two of the better boarding schools and had, for all intents and purposes, grown up on the estate shores of Miami's Biscayne Bay, he had invented for himself a new persona: fast-risen street kid from New York, language peppered with shtetl-Yiddish expressions neither of his third-generation American parents had ever heard.

Wyn had enjoyed her early days at Brown, content with the quiet literary set. Her plan had been to go on to graduate school and then instruct college students in the sedate raptures of Jane Austen. That all went kaboom when Nick discovered and electrified her with his black seen-everything-done-everything eyes and razzle-dazzle performance.

He dumped her four years after their marriage (and on the day he passed his law boards); four years of Wyn playing Galatea to his Pygmalion. She had been his creation: the ultimate in WASPdom. Old goyish family, don't you know, Nick would confide to his cronies.

Nick's old nongoyish family had disapproved of Wyn. "My dear," Audrey had said to anyone who would listen in a sub-rosa whisper meant to be heard in Sheboygan, "she's a nobody; a nothing. I'll grant you she's good looking in an eccentric way. Her innocence *is* charming even if one doesn't quite believe it. But she has no money. No name. No past. No present. No future, far as I can tell. When you think of the girls who threw themselves at Nick's feet . . ."

Audrey finally decided that if Nick wanted to stay married to Little Miss Henny Penny, *très bien*. If Nick wanted to go to law school, *très bien*. He'd have to put himself through it. She was counting on Nick's famed inability to earn a penny. But she had dismissed Wyn too quickly.

Nick and Wyn set up light housekeeping in the West Side condo Audrey had bought him lest he have no shelter. They lived on the allowance Audrey gave him lest he go hungry or unclad.

Wyn had received her real estate agent's license in no time and went to work for Nick's untasty cousins' West Side realty firm. She succeeded nicely, making enough to get Nick through Columbia Law and pay his Harmonie Club dues. ("Fellow has to make contacts somewhere.")

After the dumping, he married the daughter of the principal partner of the star-studded law firm that had hired him. Audrey then relented, welcoming him and the new bride back into the Meyer family hierarchy.

By some inexplicable twist of logic, it had been expected that Wyn would remain there as well, a morganatic ex-wife, situated on some lowly rung just above the infamous Manhattan Realtor cousins and below the psychiatric social worker daughter.

Having received her own law degree (NYU) and re-established residence as well as her father's realty office in Waggs Neck Harbor, Wyn fought long and insultingly hard to be included out. But the Meyers' philosophy and attitude never changed: She was one of them. Wyn knew that she could be a serial cannibal rapist and the Meyers would hire Dershowitz to defend her and fight for Jodie Foster to play her in the film.

Audrey Meyer continued to send well-heeled potential clients to Wyn in order, Wyn decided, to keep her terms of indenture up to date. Among Wyn's acknowledged failings was her sheer joy in earning money. So when Audrey called, Wyn—despite her best resolves—found herself listening.

Mr. Nicholas, the housekeeper said, had decided to take a run on the beach and would meet Ms. Lewis at the appointed time at the house in question.

This could be anywhere from right on the dot to never, but Wyn decided as long as she was here, she might as well pretend to go through with the showing. No matter what Nick or anyone else had to say, Audrey would eventually buy Shadows if her mood was right.

Even so, Wyn was not thrilled to be approaching Shadows again. The rain began to get serious as the windshield wipers slowed down thanks to the eccentricities of the Jaguar's electrical system. Providentially, the gates were open but as Wyn drove through, her heartbeat accelerated and bad vibrations asserted themselves.

She had the keys that Petro's nephew-heir had sent her. He had also given her the provisional listing until the estate was probated, when "perhaps a more Southamptonish Realtor might take over." Wyn wondered if she was going to be able to get her ex-mother-in-law to make an offer before the "more Southamptonish" Realtor got the listing. Split commissions were not high on Wyn's list.

She thought about waiting in the car. Being cooped up in the two-seater with the rain leaking in and claustrophobia rearing its ugly snake head decided her against it.

Nick, that macho runner in the rain, would be coming up from the beach anyway, she reasoned. Might as well get out of the rain, stop being such a chicken, and go into the house and open the oceanfront doors for him.

"Don't be ridiculous," Wyn told herself when she noticed the hand that held the key was shaking. She went on to tell herself to get serious as she walked through the dark downstairs of the rightly named Shadows. The only way the strangler would know she was there was if it were Nick, she told herself. Or if the strangler had followed her. Or if, say, Mike Bell called the office and Liz told him where she was.

She returned rapidly from unlocking the beachfront doors through the dark central corridor, past the staircase where she saw, in her mind's eye, Petronella neatly dead, her neck swathed in navy-blue panty hose. She wondered if she could convince the nephew to reinstate the electricity. Shadows—the falling-down, overpriced scene of a recent murder—was going to be difficult to show, let alone sell, without some lighting.

She didn't want to wait in the oversized foyer with Petro's ghost so she went into the forty-foot-square space Petro had called, in her advertisements, "the living chamber." That particular bit of real estate argot would no longer do, Wyn decided, supposing she would have to employ the lah-de-dah description, "drawing room." Plain old "living room" seemed an understatement.

One of the front window shutters had several broken louvers, which let in a creepy light and a sudden disturbing flash of red movement. Wyn went to the window and her blood coagulated: A small red car was parking next to her Jaguar.

A bubble-suited shape emerged. Wyn bit her lips, trying not to indulge in a tempting but impractical fit of screaming. Telling herself to get a grip, she pressed the appropriate numbers on her cellular phone. She was attempting to reach Tommy on his, cursing herself for not knowing how to use the direct dial feature that had seemed too tedious to master at the time of purchase.

I'm going to be strangled, Wyn thought, because I was too lazy to read instructions. The real American tragedy. She was greeted by an automated computer chip informing her that the cell phone customer hadn't chosen to turn on his phone at that moment.

She dialed Homer while she fought panic, remembering other times when her fear had betrayed her. She contemplated running up the stairs and finding a closet, but the idea of engaging in hide-and-seek with a mad strangler in a Waggs Neck Harbor five-and-ten bubble suit didn't play. She'd rather greet her assailant face to face than be uncovered by him in some dark attic.

Yolanda answered Homer's phone just as the visitor, standing on the porch, took off his plastic helmet and revealed himself. "Sorry, wrong number," Wyn said into the phone, remembering that was the title of an old movie about a woman trapped in a house.

"LeRoy, you scared me." Wyn left the dubious sanctity of the house to join LeRoy Stein on the huge, covered half circle of a front porch. The downspouts seemed to have failed; rain poured all around them, making Wyn feel as if she and her old friend were under a huge umbrella.

"What are you doing here?"

"Don't know," LeRoy said in his telegraphic style. It was never a good sign when he employed it; Wyn much preferred his rambling mode. With water dripping off his plastic protection, his usually distinct features dulled and aged by the water and the grim light, Wyn thought LeRoy probably resembled the displaced person his father had once been.

"Been interviewed, if that's the word for it, by the West Sea police," he went on. "They think I did in Petro and that Carruthers person. Left feeling unbearably dispirited what with the rain and my prospects. Thought I'd come over and see the old house. Lived here for a few happy moments when Ma thought we were still rich. Poor lamb."

He stopped for a moment and looked at Wyn. "Spotted the Jag. Hard to miss. Knew you were here. Thought what a splendid opportunity this was."

"For what?" Wyn asked as LeRoy advanced a step and a sopping Nick came jogging through the house.

"Vei ihz mihr, doesn't anyone ever clean this dump?" Nick examined the bottom of his now-dirty, pedicured bare feet, then looked up at Wyn and LeRoy, both immobilized. "Don't tell me you're still wearing that *shmatte* from school, Wyn. Hey, if you need money, babe, to get yourself some clothes . . . I mean people are probably going around saying, 'Nick Meyer's ex can't show her face, the clothes she's forced to wear.' I'll get my secretary to open you an account at Bergdorf's and maybe Allison can spend a day with you . . ."

"Nick, I don't want a clothing allowance from you, and as delightful as your wife is, I have no intention of spending a day with her looking for clothes that will make you look good. Try and get this through your thick head, Nick: I am no longer your wife. I belong to another. It doesn't matter what I wear or don't wear. No one in the world except you and yours thinks of me as connected in any way to you."

"How'd you like the calla lilies I sent you for your birthday?"

"I threw them in the garbage. I hate calla lilies."

"Since when?"

"Since you alerted your firm's florist to begin sending them to me."

"You want me to tell my ma that Shadows would be ideal for her guest house, don't you?" Nick asked, trying a new tack.

"No. I want you to tell her whatever you honestly think. Though she knows and you know that property-wise Shadows is one of the last great bargains on the beach."

"Can't resist the sales *schtick*, can you? You got a towel in your car, preferably soft and thick? I'm soaked all the way through. Better yet, drive me back to the house. I'll change and we'll get a bite to eat somewhere. Where's the *schlemiel* in the alien nation suit going?" With a wave of his plastic-gloved hand, LeRoy was driving off.

"I may have just discovered something," Wyn said.

"Like what?" Nick asked, following her down treacherous steps to the Jaguar.

"None of your business."

"Unlock the passenger door."

"Not likely."

"How the hell am I going to get back to my mother's?"

"The way you came."

"You'll never forgive me, will you, Wyn? Listen, come to the welcome-home dinner we're giving Ma," he called as he began to run backward toward the beach. "A major party. Allison will call with the details. You can borrow something to wear from her."

Wyn wondered, and not for the first time, if Nick were really mind-bogglingly offensive or if he just got off on irritating her.

"That *shaygets*, your carpenter husband, he can come, too."

Wyn rolled up the window and drove off, giving herself full marks for not giving in and driving him home, or telling him that a certain West Sea detective would almost certainly credit him with having saved her life.

Chapter

20

A FEW MINUTES INTO THE INTERVIEW, PASKO REALIZED HIS mistake. They had so successfully presented themselves as a single unit that he had bought into the inseparable act. "You know what," he said, glancing out the inoperable window at the rain, then looking back at them a bit desperately, "I think I'd better talk to you guys one at a time."

"Why?" Merrie asked, not one to be put off by policemen.

"Like I think the interview will go better if I talk to each of you alone."

"We don't *have* to be here, Detective," Merrie said in her tight-lipped Anglo drawl, rearranging the yellow pads on Pasko's desk, lining up his ballpoint pens.

His feet were behind and not on the desk, his shirt was buttoned, his knit tie was where it was meant to be, and he wore his gabardine jacket. He had been alerted to the fact that Merrie was major money, an important contributor to causes and politicians who tickled her fancy.

"Sweet pie," she said to Frank. "How would you feel . . . ?"

"Merrie, it's cool. If the man wants to interview us separately, let him interview us separately for God's sake."

"You have one of your headaches," Merrie accused, and Pasko thought he saw tears in the older sibling's small eyes. All this emotion was giving him a pain in the butt, but one of the cornerstones of his faith in the personal interview was the belief that important information often came out of high-strung women during their "moments."

"Nothing that aspirin can't cure," Frank said, playing down the headache and Merrie's concern. "Merrie, you go first. I'll sit in the outer office and hit on the receptionist."

"You'd better not." Merrie patted her brother's hand as Frank stood up and went out to the reception room, shutting the door behind him. Pasko wished he had more time to sort out his reactions. There was a situation here that confused him. Maybe it was that "hitting on the receptionist" routine. This brother and sister were acting, publicly, as if they were just another normal couple in love, prey to the full range of sweetheart ailments. It's sick, Pasko thought, waiting to see if Merrie would break the silence first.

She had plenty of strength, physical and emotional, and he had the feeling she could wait him out if she wanted to. And she had that snobby British accent that made Pasko want to laugh and touch his forelock at the same time.

Just as he was about to speak, Merrie took charge, asking, "What's up?" She was big and solid, built like the brick shithouse of yore. "I don't have time or energy to waste answering futile questions, Detective. Do you believe that either Frank or I killed Mrs. St. Cloud or Mrs. Carruthers?"

"It's one possibility," Pasko said, getting into character, trying to regain control. "We'll take you first. You got a motive and no alibi for the times the women were killed. When Mrs. St. Cloud bought it, you told the local police you were riding around in the country, looking for yard sales which you didn't find."

"Those blasted fools who write the yard sale advertisements should be strung up on a telephone pole. Could it possibly hurt if they gave directions or a phone number?"

"When Mrs. Carruthers was killed, you were out in your vehicle again, looking, you said, for your brother."

"He was distraught over Myra Stein's death. When he gets that way I don't know what to do. I was so worried, Frank driving around in the dark in that fast auto. You know these roads. He might have—"

As this didn't seem to be going anywhere interesting, Pasko interrupted. "The researchers have linked you to the current victims as well as to a pair of other women killed some years ago."

Merrie looked reasonably interested. "What on earth is my motive?"

"The best: money. Petronella St. Cloud and Kathy Carruthers were silent partners in the duck farm development deal with you and your brother. There was an unpublicized agreement between the four of you, drawn up by Penny McFee, witnessed by Harriet Leverage. It took a researcher days going through the village, county, and state files to come up with it." He said the latter as if it were Merrie's fault.

"I'm sorry you're wasting citizens' money with such

profligacy," Merrie said, unperturbed. "This is tedious, Detective. Do you mind if we cut to the chase?"

"All right," he agreed. His interview techniques weren't working so there was no reason not to. "Here's the working hypothesis: When McFee and Leverage realized something wasn't kosher with the duck farm deal . . ."

"What wasn't kosher?"

"Listen, Petronella St. Cloud was vice-chair of the zoning board that put the kibosh on the duck farm and later she served on the duck farm development board. We call that a conflict of interest in this country, punishable by big-time fines and jail time. So, maybe you offed McFee and Leverage to keep them from blowing the whistle.

"Then when Mike Bell began making noise more recently, talking to a lawyer, you decided St. Cloud and Carruthers had to be gotten out of the way as well. Witnesses."

"For a few million dollars, Detective? Do you think I would take that chance?"

Pasko thought she might take the chance for fifty bucks. "If the whole business came out, you and your brother could go up to the university for a few years."

"I would be surprised if you can locate one prosecutor who would take on that case." Merrie stood up. "Are you going to charge me or Frank with murder, Detective?"

"No, not now."

"Very wise. This has all the markings of a desperate attempt to find a suspect." She hesitated for a few moments while Pasko silently agreed with her. "I think I'll suggest the same to your superiors."

"I haven't spoken to your brother yet."

"Nor will you." Merrie had opened the door and

was struggling into the plastic jacket of her bubble suit. "Come, Frank. We have just stopped cooperating with the police."

Pasko wondered where he had gone wrong as Merrie led Frank up the long, lonesome corridor; then he wondered if he had gone wrong.

Frank didn't like to drive unless: he was behind the wheel of his Porsche; there was no traffic; the music was loud and twangy; he had had a teeny puff of the Jamaican weed he favored.

But on this Tuesday afternoon, returning after the tedious visit to the police and completing errands in Southampton village, he had asked Merrie if she minded if he drove the Rolls.

"Dear heart, of course not," Merrie had said, glad to be of whatever service Frank desired. He could have the damn car if he wanted it, if he'd only buck up.

Accordingly, Frank was negotiating the curving and bucolic Eight Ponds of Water Road (dairy and vegetable farms), which eventually led to West Sea Road (the occasional garage and encroaching housing development), which in turn led to Main Street and the nineteenth-century redbrick house in which they lived.

"I'm glad you took the wheel," Merrie was saying. They were passing the Last Stand, which, in season, sold vegetables and melons bought at the independent supermarket and passed off as homegrown, thus justifying the extraordinary prices levied. "I don't much like driving in the rain."

" 'I get the blues when it rains.' " Frank whistled a few bars of the old song and laughed, clueing in Merrie that he had indeed smoked a joint somewhere along the way. Not that it much affected him; in fact, marijuana usually improved his driving and often his mood.

But not this day. "Are you blue, sweetie?" Merrie asked.

"Yup. Down in the depths of the ninetieth floor."

"Still mourning Myra?"

"Still mourning Myra. And Flinty. And a number of other innocent victims. Meself included." He veered off the road sharply, pulling up in the gravel parking lot of the defunct West Sea Health and Second Nature Shop. He rested his head against the ebony steering wheel. Merrie knew Frank wanted to cry and was afraid that he wouldn't. It was always worse when Frank couldn't cry.

"You know what, Merrie?"

"What?" Merrie reached for and took Frank's hand. It was so cold. She tried to warm it up between hers.

"I think maybe it's time for me to check in with Dr. Feel Good and Co."

"Are you sure, Frank?" Endless, dreary months of being alone faced Merrie, months during which she would be separated from Frank.

"Pretty sure, Merrie." Frank looked at her with his desolate coppery eyes. The brother and sister embraced, holding on as tightly, as passionately, as if they were abandoned in a hostile black sea and each was the other's life preserver.

Chapter
21

LeRoy sauntered into the outer office of Waggs Neck Harbor Realty on that Wednesday morning with his usual poise intact, as if the day before hadn't happened.

He was wearing a shawl-collared maroon smoking jacket, yellow wide-wale corduroy trousers, and a silk ascot decorated with fleur-de-lis. "Touch chilly for spring, no?" LeRoy said to Liz Lum, who had come into the outer office to greet him.

"Maybe," she allowed. "And no, LeRoy, you can't see Wyn. Not without an appointment. She's busy."

LeRoy's protest was stillborn as Heidi Lum came out of Liz's office. She exited hurriedly after saying, unnecessarily, that she had been Xeroxing schoolwork and was late. LeRoy didn't much care why or what was detaining Heidi but her mother wondered why Heidi's top was not tucked into her skirt. Liz had learned, over the years, to pay attention to such details, which often indicated Heidi's state of mind and/or grace.

LeRoy took the opportunity to open Wyn's door and look in. "Your factotum says you won't see me but I know you will."

Wyn looked up from her desk where she was—not without guilt—digesting a jelly doughnut and a 1986 Statement of Fact submitted to the state's environmental watchdog agency by the murdered enviro-attorney, Harriet Leverage.

In it, Leverage clearly stated why the Southampton duck farm property was a serious health blight to the neighboring community. Citing state and local laws, she recommended immediately terminating its current use as a breeding ground for ducks.

"Come on in, LeRoy," Wyn said, immediately realizing her faux pas by the how-could-you? expression on Liz's face. It was important not to undermine Liz's office manager's authority. There had been many discussions about this, sometimes accompanied by tears. Wyn would make it up to her in some way. She only wished Liz would hurry up and get her real estate salesperson's license so they could hire a new office manager and then they could argue about more important stuff like money.

Liz, who was capable of stewing over Wyn's insensitive action for days, immediately lost sight of it when she went to the Xerox to switch it off. The thing ate electricity but Heidi was above such economies. Liz noticed that the last facsimile of whatever Heidi was copying was still in the machine.

She lifted the cover and gasped. It was a photostat of Heidi's bountiful breasts. No wonder her top had not been tucked in.

Liz spent the rest of the morning deep in detail work, making the computer keyboard fly, trying not to speculate on how many copies Heidi had made and for whom they were meant.

"She doesn't have a tongue ring, does she?" Wyn asked later, ever Heidi's defender.

"Not yet."

"Then be thankful."

"Pardon me for asking but we are wondering—Lettie and I—what stage the history of the New Federal Inn is at. May the first will be upon us before we know it . . ." LeRoy had forsaken his morose telegraphic style and was in full, fruity tenor.

"I'll have it for you in a week," Wyn said, thinking that was maybe a possibility. She had, after all, other things on her mind. Which reminded her: "You made a quick getaway yesterday, LeRoy."

"Yes. I felt like a dunce standing there in front of your nearly nude ex. I had driven over to Shadows to indulge in a bit of sentimentality. Not to barge in on *From Here to Eternity.*"

This seemed unfair but so much of life was. Especially other people's willful interpretations of one's innocent acts. "I thought," Wyn said, looking up at the old electric clock, seeing she was late, "that you were going to take out a pair of panty hose and strangle me for real and imagined real estate crimes."

"Crossed my mind."

There followed, after this pronouncement, a moment. A quiet, crackling moment. Wyn, in the process of putting her ancient camel's hair polo coat over her shoulders, looked up at LeRoy's full-moon face. Her tummy, as usual, reacted first. Whim-whams, big time. "What does that mean, LeRoy?" she finally was able to say.

"When we lost our shirts, when the old Fiske empire came falling down, when Mother was popped into the

Bide-a-Wee, you walked away with a number of largish commissions."

This really was unjust. Wyn had not charged Myra Fiske Stein one sou for any of the long hours she had put in trying to straighten out her legal morass. After that woman's breakdown, Wyn had offered to help pay for her removal to a better facility. LeRoy had refused with an I'm-too-proud-for-charity stance.

"If you think I used your family badly—a contention at which I take enormous umbrage"—why did she go into Mother-speak whenever she was scared and angry?—"then why have you continued to use me as your Realtor?"

"You're the best. Not saying you did anything illegal. Just that you had a piece of the pie."

"Stop, LeRoy," Wyn said, losing her mother's voice and her own composure. "You're exactly like Tommy and all the other villagers who believe I sold them out when, in reality, I saved their scrawny butts. No one I ever represented was cheated in this town. Including your mother.

"Do you know that she would have been in the hoosegow if I hadn't found buyers for the properties she had mismanaged into bankruptcy. She thought that because she was a Fiske she could turn tin into gold. She was a wonderful woman, LeRoy, but she hadn't a clue. Everyone took her for every penny they could get . . . except for Flinty Jones, who was as innocent as she was."

"Mother lost everything, Wyn," LeRoy shouted so loudly, so uncontrollably that Liz came to the door. "Everything."

Wyn was not to be cowed. "No she didn't, LeRoy," she said in an even voice. "As much as you'd like to believe it, neither you nor your mother lost your friends. After Myra's stroke, there were any number of people who would have ensured she lived in comfort. It was you, LeRoy, who insisted on carrying on as if the world had turned their back on you; as if you and your mother were alone in a callous world. You weren't and you're not."

"Thank God she wasn't arrested. She was phobic about prisons. Well, so am I." LeRoy squeezed his eyes closed and then looked at her. "They're having me come to West Sea for what they call a psychological profile. Purely voluntary. Probably tell me I'm crackers. Nothing I didn't know, Wyn."

Suddenly he didn't look like Franz Josef out for a stroll. He looked pathetic, scared. Wyn's anger was reduced to a tiny ash. "You don't *have* to go, LeRoy. It's voluntary, right? As your attorney, I'll call and . . ."

"I'm going, Wyn. Otherwise they'll pester the hell out of me. Besides," LeRoy said, working at getting his spirit up, "I enjoy psychological tests."

Wyn touched his arm and looked into the minute eyes, trying to find in them the answer to the question of the day: Was he capable of killing Petro and Kathy and those other two women for revenge? She thought he might be.

But was this old friend, this village eccentric with the big schemes and the shallow pockets, capable of killing her? She didn't have an answer for that one.

She got into the polo coat, had a hurried discussion with Liz about Xeroxed tits, and went on to her meeting with Homer and Pasko.

Chapter
22

THEY WERE IN THE BACK ROOM AT BABY'S, THE DOOR CLOSED, Pasko's hip aftershave fighting a winning battle with Homer's old-fashioned antiseptic hair lotion. "The man could fit the profile," Pasko said, looking down with expectations at May Potter's steaming, cinnamon-sprinkled apple tart. He once had a girlfriend who kept him interested long after the thrill was gone with her freshly baked apple tarts.

"I thought you didn't like LeRoy as a suspect," Homer said, carefully eating his apple pie à la mode. May, co-owner and chief chef at Baby's, had gotten a real buy—perhaps an overbuy—on Peruvian apples and was consequently working her way through *The Apple Alphabet Cook Book*.

"I like him better now. He has a solid motive, he has the strength, and he had the time. Turning up at Shadows yesterday in a bubble suit when Grace Kelly here was playing at suicide, wandering around on her lonesome . . ."

"How did he know I would be there?" Wyn asked, trying not to bolt her pound cake, thinking all of May Potter's recipes must start out with one pound of sweet butter. "It was a happenstance."

"I thought you said," Homer chimed in, "that these crimes were cleverly thought out beforehand. Perfectly organized."

"Yeah. Well maybe this one wasn't. Maybe the guy's had enough practice and he decided in a burst of wild impetuosity to whack her when he saw her Jag turn into the driveway."

"I don't believe it," Wyn said.

"Because you don't want to," Pasko returned, with Ping-Pong speed.

"What about Mike Bell?" Homer asked.

"You're like a mutt with a bone, Homer. What about Bell? He's got kind of an alibi and if you can tell me how that bozo could sound like a lady . . . both dead Realtors' receptionists swear it was a broad who made the appointments."

"I can tell you how Mike Bell could sound like a woman," Wyn said, using her forefinger to gather up the pound cake crumbs, making Homer appreciate his children's nice manners.

"Yeah?"

"I can tell you, Pasko, how *you* can sound like a woman. You get a friend—an accomplice, I believe it's called—and you give her a quarter and point her to a phone booth . . ."

"I'll eat my gun if the guy we're looking for isn't a loner."

"Or," Wyn went on instructively, "you purchase a contraption at Radio Shack for forty-nine ninety-five that can change your telephone voice into anything from a bullfrog to a mezzo-soprano."

While Wyn went to find May Potter and another slice of pound cake, Pasko dialed West Sea on his cell phone and told the techies to check the two tapes he had brought in for machine-interfered voices. Seeing Homer's irritating smile, Pasko barked: "Yeah, she's a regular Nancy Drew, ain't she?"

"And you do know why there was no sign of humanity at the crime scenes?" Wyn said, returning, pushing her luck.

"The famous bubble suits," Pasko retorted. "This year's fashion statement for compulsive stranglers. Hardly leaves a trace of porch dust in the house. Available for the last twenty years at your local dime store. Forensic techies have been wearing shit like that for years so as not to pollute crime scenes. This is not news, Ms. Handwerk."

"Frank Jones," Homer said, moving things along and sorry Wyn hadn't won that round.

"Same great real estate motive," Pasko allowed. "Father given a royal fuck-over and left for dead by the real estate vultures."

Before Wyn could say anything, Homer—resigned to the role of mediator—said, "Frank's too puny."

"What?" Pasko asked.

"You heard me," Homer said. "Frank's too puny. According to the forensic report your boss was kind enough to send me—PS, he wants to talk to you about your sense of cooperation—the killer was bigger than the victims."

"So Frankie stood on a step and threw the panty hose around the necks of his victims. It would give him an advantage and his rage would give him the strength. He's got half an alibi for the Carruthers murder and only his sister's word for where he was when Mrs. St. Cloud was buying hers.

"He's also a certifiable loony. Periodically, he checks in to get his clock reset. I asked the main man at his rest home, some yutzo with an accent, why poor disturbed Frankie was allowed to run around on our public streets and the guy had the nerve to hang up on me."

"My," Wyn said. "You've been busy."

"I got a great researcher."

"So why don't you arrest Frank? Or Mike? Or LeRoy Stein?" Homer asked, knowing the answer.

"Because we haven't got a goddamned thing on any of them that would stand up in court. We got to nab the fucker in the act."

He looked at Wyn. Homer, who didn't want to, looked at Wyn as well. "And the weekend is coming up. We could put you in a jail cell, Ms. Lewis, until Sunday, which would have him/her crapping in their shorts . . . these ritual numb nuts like to keep on schedule. A lot of effort was put into making us believe Carruthers got hers on a Saturday morning. But there'll always be another weekend and . . ."

"Not a chance," Wyn said, getting up, grabbing her coat and what was left of her cake, and leaving.

"She's fine," Pasko said. "Man, isn't she fine? That hair, and those eyes and that nice, trim body in those weird outfits. You got to admit, Midnight, that she is . . ."

"Fine." Homer stood up and went to the lone, narrow window in the room that had once been used, when the building was a mortician's residence, to house coffins. The view was of the village parking lot, bereft of cars or significant greenery, puddles of water left from the weekend rain competing with pools of engine oil. "Do you think Mike Bell, or whoever it is, is going to try to kill her?"

169

"I do," Pasko said, sensing an unlikely ally. "She figures, in one way or another, in every one of these deals. I think she may even be the principal target. That he/she has held off on icing her because she's dessert. I think that unless she cooperates, or unless we're lucky—and let's face it, Midnight, we're not lucky guys—the bastard's going to do her and evaporate.

"Why don't you talk to her? She likes you. She'll believe you when you tell her we won't let him get to her."

There was no response. Homer was staring at something in the parking lot. Pasko joined him. Wyn, who had stopped to talk to May Potter, had just reached the Jaguar. She had opened the driver's door but wasn't getting in. After a long moment, she stepped back and then aside like a model at a car show.

The two men inside Baby's could see something stringy and odd wrapped around Wyn's steering wheel. It took them a moment to realize what it was.

They reached her as she was undoing a pair of midnight-blue panty hose. "Wyn," Homer said, touching her shoulder. She looked at him with her sublimely innocent face, one hand holding the obscene panty hose, the other reaching for his. She turned to look at Pasko and if he hadn't realized before, he did now. She really, really didn't like him. "Just how, Pasko, do we set me up?"

"I don't like it," Tommy said later, from the depths of the green sofa. This was after the wiretaps had been installed down at the office and in the basement of their home; after the ad had been placed in the Waggs Neck Harbor *Chronicle*.

"Nobody *likes* it, Tommy," Wyn said, joining him, feeling irrationally relieved. A part of her had recognized—ever since Pasko first had hinted at it—that she was going to end up as prime fillet for the lion. And here she was, shrink-wrapped and date-stamped, ready to be placed in the meat case.

She herself had written the advertisement that was to run in the weekend real estate section of the *Chronicle:*

AN INVESTMENT OPPORTUNITY NOT TO BE MISSED! The old watch factory is on the market and this time the owners say SELL SELL SELL at any price. For a private Saturday viewing, call Wyn Lewis at Waggs Neck Harbor Realty on Main Street.

"No," Tommy said to himself, putting his arm around her, moving close. The only illumination in the room came from a streetlight reflecting off the glass in the French doors. Probity was at their feet. It was cozy and womb-y and all Wyn wanted to do was hunker down and bliss out.

"I'm not talking about the big picture," Tommy went on. "I'm talking about the panty hose around the steering wheel. It's out of character."

"You've been watching too many episodes of *N.Y.P.D. Blue.* Maybe it was a warning, or a new move to up the suspense. It would seem to be the least of my troubles at this moment."

"All right. Let's put it and the murders and your acting as the bait clean out of our minds."

"Not likely."

"I have an idea that will help."

Later, as they lay nude and cocooned in the depths

171

of the sofa, Wyn had to admit that Tommy's idea had helped; but still, in the hurricane of her mind, deep down at the calm, relentless bottom of the eye, was the knowledge that someone was going to try to strangle her, and she, poor dope, was doing everything she could to help.

Chapter

23

MIKE BELL LAY IN THE WIDE BED IN THE NARROW ROOM HE inhabited in the New Federal attic amazed by the fact that twenty minutes after sex, he was ready again. "You horny bastard," he said to himself affectionately, inhaling—with gusto—the contrasting smells of sweat and sex.

Lettie had left a quarter of an hour before in a swirl of Balenciaga sleepware and Miss Dior perfume and an admonishment he musn't be late to take over the front desk.

When Lettie finally agreed to marry him, he was going to have to make damn sure she never knew about his other bedmates; and, more critical, he was going to have to teach her that if she wanted staff behind the front desk at nine in the morning, she was going to have to hire them. Or fill in herself. Do the bitch good.

If Lettie never agreed to marry him—and Mike was astute enough to know that was a possibility—he was banking on real estate school. He thought he could do pretty well in real estate, considering the competition. He didn't think much of Wyn Lewis's marketing techniques. Like she didn't have any.

He looked at his new chrome watch (Lettie could have sprung for gold) and then at himself in the mirrored wall she had installed. " 'You big, mean, hairy ape,' " he mimed Lettie's last words to him. " 'I'm afraid you're terribly attractive.' " He had to agree he was hairy. He wondered if he needed another shave, rubbing his hand over his cheek, deciding he did but he wouldn't. His women seemed to like beard burn.

He gathered up the damp sheets and stashed them under the bed where his sister, the maid of the moment (Lettie did run through staff), would find them. He threw a new sheet over the thin mattress, took a fast, invigorating shower, and was back in bed, ready for action, keeping his mind busy with the real estate course manual chapter on full disclosure, when the agreed-upon surreptitious knock came.

He told her to come on in. She threw the Friday *Chronicle* over his privates. He opened it while she undressed. The Xerox of her tits had been folded into the sports section. As attention-grabbing as this was, he was more interested in Wyn's ad.

While Heidi had her way with him, Mike read it over twice before putting the paper down, a little surprised.

"You losing interest?" Heidi wanted to know.

"Does this look like I'm losing interest?" Mike asked, still pondering the various implications of Wyn's ad.

Frank and Merrie Jones were sitting at the breakfast table drinking decaf, nibbling at croissants, and going over the real estate sections of the various local papers. This was their habit on a Friday morning when new

174

ads appeared and desperate homeowners broadcast their plight by announcing important markdowns.

Merrie was, not unexpectedly, methodical in her perusals. "Hear this, dear heart," she said to Frank, who seemed to have lost a once exuberant interest in the subject. Frank had put aside his copy of *The East Hampton Star*—Merrie was too particular about paper folds to read someone else's newspaper—and was indolently petting the yellow street cat he had adopted. Merrie did not like cats but if the cat amused Frank, so be it.

She read Wyn's ad aloud, with appropriate vibrato, and was pleased to see that Frank had perked up. "You know, dearie, it might be fun to do the watch factory," Merrie said, wondering if this tasty realty dish could tempt Frank out of his depression. "Maybe we should go look at it with Wyn."

"Maybe *I* should," Frank said, feeding the yellow alley cat decaf from a silver spoon.

Lettie was enjoying late breakfast with LeRoy in the New Federal's narrow, glass-enclosed side dining porch, going over plans for the fast-approaching centennial celebration of the founding of her hotel. LeRoy, who had his own problems, couldn't help but notice that Lettitia was looking positively ripe. She edged her chair an inch to the left so she could have a full view of the lobby, the bar, and Main Street. In her next life, LeRoy decided, Lettie would be a periscope.

From her vantage point, Lettie could see that Mike, that darling slug-a-bed, had not yet taken his place behind the front desk. His nymphomaniacal sister was there in his place when she should have been upstairs cleaning the guest rooms. It was Friday and the weekenders would be arriving in a few hours, looking forward to rum punches in the Jacuzzis and nouvelle cuisine in the dining room.

Well, Lettie decided, the poor boy had worked long and hard this morning and could be excused just this once. Still, she couldn't wait for the day when she lost interest in the Mike Bells of this world and could concentrate on her real passions: longevity and money.

LeRoy had finished presenting his plans for the hotel's centennial luncheon party up in the Rooftop Café. "All schools, religious organizations, historical societies, et cetera, have agreed to participate in the preluncheon parade. Media interest is intense. The *Times* is especially interested. We may get a Sunday feature and not just in the Long Island section."

"Are you broke, LeRoy?" Lettie asked, incapable of believing anyone could look as down as LeRoy for other than fiscal reasons.

"More or less."

"Well, after the centennial, we'll have to see about finding you something to do. Something remunerative. Do you need money immediately?"

"No, Lettie, I can hold out."

Lettie had a deserved Madame Scrooge reputation but she was aware that her late brother had bought the hotel for next to nothing thanks to LeRoy's family's downfall and that she in turn had inherited a gold mine. Timing and taste, Phineas used to say, was all.

Myra Fiske Stein, sweet dope, had neither. "What happened to the ten grand I lent you before you left for Florida?" Lettie asked LeRoy. "Elizabeth Bishop, the poet, you know, said Florida was the state with the prettiest name but I've always preferred Virginia. Or Georgia. My producer has been talking about my doing a one-woman Elizabeth Bishop tour on the university circuit but let's face facts: Do they know who she was?"

The subject of the loan had not come up before, as it had been manifest that LeRoy had returned to the village with only stories of his Florida success and nothing to back them up.

"I was taken," LeRoy finally admitted, knowing full well who Elizabeth Bishop was but not, at this moment, much caring. He was looking into his coffee cup, seeing nothing but darkness.

"Let's say that we'll consider half the loan a payment for your handling of the centennial and later, we can talk about ways of your working off the rest." Lettie felt she was being generous . . . there was no point in going overboard. "Perhaps you could be the hotel general manager. You're good with people and detail work and I'm thinking of traveling a bit.

"Dear Mike has never been to Europe, can you imagine? Fact is, he's never been anywhere. Maybe he and I could combine business with pleasure. I could do the Elizabeth Bishop thing and Mike could be the chief gofer. Even if they haven't heard of Elizabeth what's-her-name, they've heard of me. Or maybe I could do alternate nights. Edith Wharton every other performance . . ."

Lettie went on blithely while LeRoy was mired in memories of the disaster that was Florida.

He had bought into a new and what was to him exciting concept: a condominiumized trailer camp just west of wishfully named Frost Free, halfway down the peninsula and an equal distance from either coast.

His partners were a pair of retired military men from Birmingham, Alabama, who had been searching for a junior partner with ten thousand dollars who was willing to oversee the operation. LeRoy had answered their ad in *The Wall Street Journal.*

They met in Frost Free and explored the trailer camp site and conferenced with the elderly midwestern renters who were to be convinced to buy their trailers. The deal was signed in a weekend.

LeRoy had brought with him an ancient Land Rover and was lent a prefabricated house a few miles from the camp that would have depressed him if he hadn't draped scarfs over all the lampshades, lending atmosphere to the drab rooms.

On his first Monday, the camp's pool waters turned lime green. The original pool contractor had folded. The Florida Pool Association's nearest office recommended a consultant. This thin, grizzled fellow had driven over from Tampa and concluded that the pool was a disaster. The concrete had been mixed with saltwater, the filters had rotted out, and the liner had developed a number of leaks. To repair the pool would cost twenty thousand dollars; to replace it would cost fifteen.

On Tuesday, the electricity went. A disgruntled, pool-obsessed tenant had sabotaged the main wires leading to the camp. On Wednesday, there was a suspicious fire in two of the empty units fronting the mosquito-infested swamp.

LeRoy arrived at six in the morning to see if he could help put out the fire, parking his Land Rover in front of the trembling trellis that bore the camp's name and hopeful motto: "Sunset Park. A New Direction in Down-Home Retirement Living."

After talking with the firemen and attempting without any luck to get in touch with his partners, he left Sunset Park at sunrise and went to his vehicle.

The trailer rentees had all lined up on the far side of the dusty road. They stood under the sparse shade of the Australian pines the Birmingham men had planted in a mistaken attempt to provide the project with curb appeal. The alien pines were drinking up all the available water and multiplying like jackrabbits. The county said they had to be rooted out, pronto.

It was a scorcher of a day, but nothing equal to the restrained heat of the disenchanted elderly who stood staring at LeRoy with naked hate.

LeRoy smiled at this hostile audience, holding out his hands in a placating gesture. "It will be put to rights in the morning," he said, getting into the Land Rover, praying it would start, smiling encouragingly, backing up over the balding trailer camp dog who had taken refuge from the sun in the shade of the car. He studied the dog in his rear-view mirror, decided it was dead and that no good could come from trying to resurrect it. He drove off as the crowd booed.

In the morning, only the dog's carcass remained. All of the condominium prospects were gone, back to Dayton or Cuyahoga Falls or wherever they belonged. LeRoy managed to coax the Land Rover to Miami Beach, where he sold it and got a job as an assistant manager in a seedy, small hotel.

Vividly remembering that sad state of affairs, thinking of the fruitless eons he was going to be indentured to Lettie, regretting again his mother's last years, LeRoy was suffused with a feeling much like hate.

"What's the matter with you?" Lettie asked, seeing LeRoy's face go red, then green, like an out-of-control traffic light. "You'd best not be having a stroke in my hotel, LeRoy Stein."

"No," LeRoy said, looking through the panes of the glass wall toward Waggs Neck Harbor Realty. "I'm merely having a vivid fantasy of revenge."

"Phew. For a moment I thought we were going to have to have doctors and ambulances and such. Friday morning is not the optimal time for someone to suffer a stroke in the hotel. The thought of those men in the poison-green intern suits running through the lobby makes my heart stop. You're quite certain you're all right?"

Lettie may have been textbook egotistical but she could and did have some feeling for LeRoy. He was so like his mother, misguided but essentially good. Carefully examining his unhealthy skin again and deciding he was not going to cause a medical emergency, Lettie missed the sight of Heidi slipping down the rear stairs and out the parking lot door.

"Who were you having revenge against?" Lettie asked.

"Ruthless Realtors," LeRoy said as Wyn Lewis exited from her real estate office across the street.

Chapter

24

"GIVE ME A BREAK, LIZ. WHAT MAKES YOU THINK," WYN asked, "that those two creatures could protect me from a field mouse much less Petro's and Kathy's killer?"

"Now, listen, Wyn."

"I'm listening, Liz."

"No you're not. Whenever you put on that voice and that face, I know you're not paying attention. Trouble with you has always been the same old, same old: You were born one of the high and mighty of the village and though you deny it, you and the Carlsons and the Littlefields and the Coles . . . you all still think your poop doesn't smell. That's why Nick Meyer dumped you, if you want to know the Truth."

"Spare me the Truth, Liz."

"No matter how high he climbed, he knew you would always look down on him for not being the WASP your father was."

"Oh, Lord. Anna Freud has descended on Waggs

Neck Harbor Village. Liz, would you please stop. You come from the same kind of family . . ."

"Oh, no I don't. We were always poor. You were always rich. We lived in a pokey house on the flats. You lived on the hill."

"It's a tiny hill, Liz."

"Nonetheless, we had to look up to you. You and your perfect daddy, not to mention complexion, and getting into Brown, and even when your marriage to the exotic Jewish prince went down the tubes you came back here not with your tail between your legs . . ."

". . . such a stunning visual . . ."

". . . but with a law degree and a Realtor's license and in twenty minutes you were minting money selling broken-down houses and the only man in town anyone ever wanted was kissing your size five double A feet. You have no idea how much I've hated you, Wyn Lewis."

"I do now." Wyn mimed talking into a microphone. "Liz the Wuss, everyone, has emerged from the hostility closet, on the attack."

They looked at one another with as much rancor as either could dredge up and then Liz Lum started to laugh. " 'Liz the Wuss,' " she said, doubling over.

Wyn found herself laughing, too. They had been friends since kindergarten when Liz, towering over Wyn then and now, had protected her from the Water Street bullies.

At this moment they were closeted in Liz's small, windowless office. Every surface unoccupied by jocose penguins was piled high with real estate textbooks and motivational tapes. Liz was hoping to pass the upcoming real estate exam for salesmen. "Now that I've given up sex, and vice versa, I want to be rich, too," she said.

"I want to sell out this village like no one has ever sold it out before."

Wyn, feeling *she* was being sold out, reverted to the subject that had set Liz off in the first place: Who was to accompany her on the showing?

It was Friday afternoon and a request had come in to see a Robins Way "bungaloid." Bungaloid was the description Wyn gave the new-built-to-look-old micro-range-equipped cottages dangerous developers were popping up in the middle of the straggly old pine forest.

They were marketed mostly for villagers who had sold their appealing but desperately in need of repair nineteenth-century gingerbreaded houses for what they would maintain to the grave was half of what they were worth. Complete with in-home vacuum-cleaning systems and self-cleaning ovens, the bungaloids were a grand success.

Wyn had sworn to Homer, Pasko, and most especially to Tommy, that she wouldn't go on a showing alone until the perp (they were all talking like characters from TV) was arrested.

On the other hand, Wyn did not want to drag Tommy all the way back from East Hampton and Homer was in West Sea, again meeting with Pasko's boss, Captain Savage. The other possibility for protection, Pasko, was out of the question.

As yet, no one had responded to the baited ad. The present showing seemed innocent enough since the killer apparently favored large, empty structures, not tarted-up tract housing, for his murders. Thus, when Wyn had asked Liz to come up with a suitable attendant, Liz suggested Dickie ffrench and his septuagenarian aunt-in-law, Lucy Littlefield.

"Wyn, you didn't say they had to have muscles and

sawed-off machine guns. And whoever he is, if the strangler sees three of you, he'll skedaddle."

Wyn allowed, ungraciously, that she supposed Liz was right. There was safety in numbers and anyway none of the other pieces fit: The house she was showing was not a desolate mansion; this was not Saturday morning but Friday afternoon; a man, not a woman, had requested the showing.

"Want me to drive, Wyn?" Lucy asked hopefully, having long wanted to get her mittened hands on the Jaguar.

Wyn diplomatically said certainly but she supposed they'd better take Lucy's car as three was a tight squeeze in hers. Lucy's vehicle was a 1950-something Dodge sedan that boasted pushbutton shifting and a lack of springs. "We could walk," Lucy ventured, looking down affectionately at the beaded, pink Indian moccasins she had bought from the Seminole tribe in Everglades City, Florida, circa 1946.

Dickie said "not in this life" to the prospect of walking. In the end they drove in Lucy's car, Lucy putting forefinger to parched lips each time she had to decide which button to push to shift.

The bungaloid was in a subdivision known as Mockingbird Hill. It was, like every third house on the new, unlandscaped Robins Way, vinyl-sided in cheery yellow with nonworking white vinyl shutters and a goodly amount of galvanized drain piping. It was being resold two months after the initial closing due to a precipitous divorce.

Wyn placed Dickie and Lucy in the living room on a plastic-protected Castro convertible covered in a yellow and white synthetic fabric Dickie said he wouldn't use to sneeze into. Half a dozen throw pillows complemented the sofa's unforgiving foam rubber cushions. The house, Dickie said, looking around, should have been named as correspondent.

"Just be quiet," Wyn said to Dickie, including Lucy in her range of malice. "If either of you queer this deal, I'm going to make you pay me my commission."

"Let's not forget why we are here, Wynsome dear," Lucy said, taking the high tone. "Or the sacrifices we are making *for you.* Jane and Baby ffrench are having to hold down the shop so we can be here *with you.* We understand your nerves are a touch tentative but a teeny-weeny attempt at graciousness might not be inappropriate."

"Amen," Dickie added. They all knew the only reason he and Lucy were there: Besides their basic Good Samaritanism, there was a possibility of catching sight of the strangler. They could dine out on the story for decades.

Still, it was boring sitting in this antiseptic, tacky living room with Dickie being evil. Lucy wondered if she dared ask Wyn if she might be allowed to click on the TV. The *Golden Shower Hour of Bath Essentials* was just beginning on the shop-at-home channel and Lucy had long had her eye on a gilded cupid soap dish. Taking in Wyn's wintry demeanor, Lucy regretfully decided not.

Wyn, discovering cat feces in the master bedroom suite, unceremoniously took two of the sofa's throw pillows and threw them down as cover, spraying the room with the owner's Van Gogh cologne.

"You sure are a dervish of activity," Lucy felt obliged to comment. Wyn was closing commode seats, pulling up Levolors, switching on lights, playing elevator music on the stereo system, and, in general, prepping the house.

"Minute the prospect pulls up, you two go out on the front porch and sit on the swing."

"It's made of rubber tires," Dickie objected.

"It won't contaminate you," Lucy said. "And it will be fun. We'll swing on the swing and try to look like hip, happy homeowners."

"If we're so hip and happy," Dickie wanted to know, "why are we selling?"

"A death in the family," Wyn offered as she heard the sound of a car displacing gravel in the driveway. She turned to the picture window where she had pushed aside the cottonlike curtains and saw a black Mustang convertible. Mike Bell was getting out of it.

"I'm previewing," Mike explained, looking out on the porch where Lucy was getting overly enthusiastic about the swinging and Dickie was turning green.

Another preview. Wyn stood in the two-foot-square entry foyer, trying to ignore the fact that the bifold closet door was off its track. "Why did you say the showing was for a person named Phil Marcus?"

"Because like that's who the preview is for, Wyn."

Mike was wearing a navy blue wool crepe Armani blazer, prefaded jeans, a white linen Nehru shirt and brown tasseled loafers. He looked pricey, like a page out of a Barney's catalog. He looked professional, though Wyn couldn't decide professional at what. "You haven't gotten your real estate license yet, have you, Michael?" she asked, feeling like a long arm of the real estate law.

"No, and I haven't passed myself off as a salesman, either. I'm just doing this summer dude who I sometimes crew for a favor. He heard about the split and that the house was going cheap and he wanted me to take a look at it for him. When I get my license, he's going to be my first prospect. You got a problem with this, Wyn?"

Wyn thought that Mike Bell, if he stuck with it and stayed honest, would make a formidable real estate salesman. He would never understand the heart and soul of an old village house; he would do best, she guessed, with low-end contemporary housing. *"No problema,"* she said after a moment, though she didn't like any of this. "Want to take a look?"

"That's what I'm here for. You got a sheet?"

Wyn handed him the information page she supplied with each showing, detailing price and footage and air conditionable/heatable space as well as potential mortgage assumability and neighborhood character.

Mike looked it over and folded it neatly, placing it into his blazer pocket. Then he whisked through the house, checking out the stack washer/dryer and asking informed questions about the efficient-looking heating/cooling system in the basement. He said thanks, went out on the porch, made an all-purpose noise that might have signified good-bye to Lucy and Dickie, and was gone.

"Think he meant to strangle you?" Lucy asked, on the drive back. "Boy's intense, isn't he?" Wyn ignored this, wondering what would have happened if she and Mike Bell had been alone in the compact basement.

"Don't you hate real men?" Dickie asked from the back seat, fanning himself with his hand, the Dodge's rear window handles long gone. "But one has to admit Mike Bell cleans up nicely. Lucky Lettie. He's marvelously attractive in a sinister sort of way. And you could imagine him strangling someone in the heat of passion. Sex and death are so closely allied, aren't they?"

Wyn returned to her office where Liz Lum announced there had been three callers inquiring about seeing the old watch factory.

Wyn called to see if Homer had returned from playing footsie with Captain Savage. Fear made her cranky. Yolanda gave her a short, hard time but eventually put her through. "Two of the calls were legit," Homer said. His sergeant, Ray Cardinal, had been monitoring them. "Only one held promise. It was from the pay phone in the hotel and probably was our man, or woman."

"We only need one," Wyn said, feeling control slipping quietly away. She did what she tried never to do and that was to call Tommy on his cellular and ask him if he could please come home early. Tommy, that pushover, said he was on his way.

Chapter

25

UNABLE TO SLEEP, WYN ARRIVED AT HER OFFICE AT SIX-THIRTY A.M. armed with a plastic cup of the Eden's malignant coffee and a cheese Danish that even Thelma Eden admitted had seen better days. "I'm giving you twenty-five cents off," Thelma had allowed. "Just this once. You can't expect fresh on Saturday, Wyn."

Wyn entered her office with tentative speed, raising the window-wide blind quickly. Thus she would be in plain view of the trio of early morning pensioners who gathered daily on the bank bench across the street and watched her window as if it were a mega-sized television in a sports bar.

Her phone rang moments after she sat down at the old partners desk. "Where the hell are you?" Tommy, who rarely cursed, asked. "Probity and I woke up and no you . . ."

"If you'll read the note on the pillow, Tommy—the one next to your head—you'll learn that I had a hard night's sleep and came down to the office where I am now under the watchful eyes of Bud Olafson and Pete Briglia and that fellow who has no name, all sitting on the bank bench . . ."

"I'll be right there."

"No you won't," Wyn said, stopping him. The last thing she needed was Tommy hanging around, watching her out of the corners of those blue eyes. "You have your role today and I have mine. Go back to sleep."

"I can't."

"Then have a bowl of your ultranutritious gruel and don't forget Probity needs a walk. Love you." She replaced the receiver, thought about calling him back, and then thought about calling Liz and Homer and her uncle in Key West, Florida, but didn't.

Instead, she found consolation and occupation by switching on the microfiche machine and wallowing in the old deeds, legal documents, odd letters, and articles of sale that told the real estate story of the New Federal Inn.

The inn had passed down through the founding family—the Fiskes—to Myra, who took over its management shortly after her immigrant husband died. When Myra was declared a 1986 bankrupt, the New Federal was sold at auction to Phineas Browne, Lettie's brother, who transformed it into a fancy and profitable hostelry. The bankruptcy, the loss of face, was said to be responsible for Myra's paralyzing stroke. Wyn wasn't so certain. Myra had had that combination of guts and benightedness that would have let her face anything.

LeRoy had inherited some of that. The village parlor therapists decided his affectations and inability to make a living were a result of his father's foreignness and his mother's mistaken belief in her own managerial capabilities. For a while the buzz around the old ladies' sitting rooms was "Pity, but that's what Myra got for marrying an outsider."

Bored with the New Federal history and characters, Wyn pulled out of her compliant computer the files relating to her first big deal, the complicated duck farm transactions. Liz had entered the new information Pasko had seen fit to share and Wyn was sad to learn that old documents still could cause dismay: She had not been Myra Fiske Stein's first choice for an attorney.

Penny McFee had. But, Wyn deduced, when the aptly named McFee had found that the legendary Fiske fortune was just that, that there were no monies available to pay her, she quietly dusted Myra off; old fee-less Wyn, friend of the family, was hired.

There was more news. Wyn was aware that Harriet Leverage had been the young prosecuting attorney working for Myra's creditors, but not that she had been, for a time, Phineas Browne's personal attorney as well. Had the saintly Harriet made it easy for Phineas to acquire the New Federal thanks to some unrecorded fiscal inducements? Had she and Penny McFee similarly smoothed the way for the new duck farm owners—Merrie and Frank—to build their obscenely profitable development?

Probably, but it didn't matter now except as one more piece of evidence that the world was a terrible place and the people in it no better than they should be.

Wyn told herself to get off the moralizing but her neurons were working full-time, making her brain a busy, painful, and uncontrollable place. Some epiphany was trying to come together: Myra and Harriet Leverage and Penny McFee and Phineas Browne and all those Bells and Merrie and Frank and LeRoy . . . It reminded her of a game she had played as a child in which saying the names of the players evoked opposing rules and recriminations. Donald: One step backward. Mary: Show us your underpants. Et cetera.

The office telephone rang and a solemn-eyed Liz, who had arrived some minutes before, came in to announce that a prospect was on the phone. "She wants to know if you can show her the watch factory in an hour's time."

Wyn, aware of the monitors in Homer's offices and Pasko's promises of superhuman surveillance, felt a new, righteous surge of anger at the pointless deaths of those four women. As the pieces of the puzzle rearranged themselves in her mind, she realized they had been killed for a variety of reasons: greed, self-protection, revenge, sportsmanship.

It was the latter that made her most furious: the fact that to the killer it was all a game; that the players who broke the rules, real or imagined, were the ones who had to die.

"Tell her," Wyn said, "that it will be my pleasure."

Chapter
26

THE EXIGENCIES OF RECENT STATE-MANDATED CUTS IN LAW enforcement funding, combined with the bloody-mindedness of Captain Savage, had forced Pasko and Homer to work together on that sun-filled Saturday morning.

Pasko was admittedly "at the end of his cork," clad in his off-duty blue jeans, graying yellow sweatshirt, basketball sneakers, and half a pint of aftershave. He'd been informed that if today didn't produce "substantial results," he was to drop the case and take up a new workload. Maybe even a new line of work.

"And like where is the case to be dropped?" Pasko had short-sightedly asked Captain Savage.

"Into the lap of one Homer Price, captain of Waggs Neck Harbor Police. He's a capable, no-nonsense policeman. I'm trying to woo him over here. Man would make a fine lieutenant detective."

"You planning to can me, Savage?" Pasko held the sole West Sea lieutenant detective slot and what with

the new, lean, mean budget, the likelihood of an opening being created was slim.

"The union will make sure you have options. You
could make a lateral move, salarywise, to the Department of Motor Vehicles. Seems you have a pal in the
DMV. Or you could stay here and be demoted to a
nice desk job, depending on your computer skills. Then
there's always early retirement. Not a bad deal for a
single guy. Though I hear rumors in the cafeteria that
bells are about to ring for you and one slightly pregnant
red-hot chili pepper."

"Would you quit twitching?" Homer asked Pasko.
Hands in trouser pockets, jingling change and car keys,
the detective was pacing around the office in the Waggs
Neck Harbor Municipal Building, where Wyn's phones
were being monitored.

Pasko looked at Homer with deep dislike. "Listen,
Negro, you don't talk to me like that . . ." Homer
pushed himself away from his desk and rose, big fists
clenched. Pasko backed away, arranging himself in
fighting stance.

There might have been some real damage if technol-
ogy hadn't kicked in at that moment. With a surprising
immediacy, as if they were in the same room, they
overheard, via the mid-quality Radio Shack speakers,
Liz Lum's deep contralto answering the Waggs Neck
Harbor Realty phone and a fruity voice asking for an
appointment to see the watch factory.

"It's coming from the New Federal's back bar
phone," Homer's recently promoted sergeant, Ray
Cardinal, said with brio, disappointed that he hadn't
seen his captain beat the shit out of Pasko.

His first assignment of the morning was to monitor
the recently acquired caller ID machine, which told, in

seconds, the numbers of callers and the location. "It's like amazing," he said to an unresponsive Pasko.

"Fuckin' amazing," Pasko returned. "Let's go."

"Sure it's the same voice?" Homer asked cautiously.

"You heard the tapes, Captain Midnight. It's *the* voice whether the perp's using a voice changer or not."

As the least known and most inconspicuous of the three, Ray was sent, double time, over to the New Federal. "See who's sitting on the phone," Pasko told him.

Homer and Pasko left the Municipal Building by the rear exit and got into Homer's wife's anonymous tan Taurus station wagon. All this without a word between them. Homer drove the car through the village parking lot to the Washington Street exit, took a left and then another left onto Main Street, and parked in the New Federal's loading zone.

Pasko broke the somber silence by asking if Homer minded if he smoked and Homer said yeah, he minded. The atmosphere was as thick as a steam room. It wasn't his fault, Pasko told himself. Now that a little heat had been let out, he was willing to be cordial.

Not Homer. Wyn once said that Homer was quick to forgive though he never forgot. That "Negro"—which, in Homer's mind might just as well have been "nigger"—would rankle for some time.

It was one of the misguided beliefs of the rough New York youth Pasko carried with him that words didn't count ("sticks and stones," etc.), that Homer Price would magically disremember the recent scene in the office. It was like over. Why dwell on it?

Moments later, Ray emerged and got into the backseat of the Taurus. All three suspects, he reported, were in the glass dining room, a fact that Pasko said didn't make eliminating any one of them too easy. The good news, Homer contended, was that they all had access to the obscure telephone booth near the restrooms that had been used to make the call so they were, finally, substantial suspects.

"Yeah, great news," Pasko said. "What were our substantial suspects doing?" he asked Ray.

"LeRoy Stein is packing away five poached eggs and what looks like a pound of bacon. Mike Bell is guzzling Pepsi Light at the bar, jumping up every time the hotel phone rings. Looks like a guy who has to take a leak, bad.

"Frank Jones is sitting with his sister. They're eating those little sweet rolls and drinking tea. Ms. Jones is reading *The Wall Street Journal*. Frank is staring out the window at I don't know what. Space, maybe.

"Only one who noticed I existed was Victoria Bell, who's playing waitress today and offered me coffee." Ray felt it was okay not to mention what else Vicky offered him. He'd already had some, anyway.

Stopping conversation in the Taurus, Mike Bell, in his new blazer, came out and stood nervously on the hotel porch. He was indeed jumpy, looking as if he were expecting the gestapo. Not finding them, he moved quickly to the side driveway, which led to the hotel's parking lot.

"Get out," Homer said to Pasko with less than his customary courtesy. By prearrangement Mike Bell was his. Believing Bell was taking a shortcut across the parking lot to the watch factory, Homer intended to pull into the driveway after him.

Before he could, Bell's mean Mustang shot out of the hotel parking lot driveway, narrowly missed the Taurus's front bumper, and made a left onto Main Street.

Homer U-turned illegally to follow Mike Bell west on Main. He wondered if this was a diversionary tactic; if Bell had seen them; if he was going to turn south off

Lower Main way down on the dirt road known locally as the Sharon Wells Turnpike, then connect up with Bay and approach the watch factory from the west.

After Bell's and the captain's speedy departures, Pasko took over. "Hey, Junior G-man," he said to Ray. "Why don't you park your truck in back of the hotel so you can be near Frank's Porsche." This was met with a blank stare. "In case," Pasko explained slowly, "Frank decides to take off via Bay Street."

Pasko had cased the hotel parking lot earlier, wondering where the Rolls was. Probably at the love nest, he decided, driving past Frank and Merrie's Lower Main Street house just to make sure. There it was, the lovely red leviathan, sitting under the porte cochere, looking like an ad in the kind of magazine Pasko never read. Rich people, he said with a mixture of disdain and envy.

"And," Ray was saying, feeling a twinge of guilt talking to his chief's arch enemy, "if Frank's planning to visit the watch factory, he could use the New Federal's back exit and walk across the parking lot."

"A-plus, Boy Wonder. What about shutting the fuck up and moving your little footsies?"

Ray Cardinal, in his immaculate 1985 blue and white Chevy pickup, watched Frank Jones come out of the back of the hotel alone and get into a car for which Ray would have forfeited his left testicle. Frank headed east on Bay Street and then south on Swamp Road, picking up speed as he went.

Communicating with Homer via cell phone, Ray, made uncharacteristically talkative by the excitement of a genuine case, wondered if everyone was into diversionary strategy today, if Frank were going to follow

Swamp Road until it hit Route 114 and then take it back to Bay Street and the factory.

"Maybe it's going to be like that old movie where they're all murderers," Ray said enthusiastically. Homer, breaking the connection, said he didn't think so.

After giving orders to Ray, Pasko had taken a seat at the New Federal's bar, wanting to make sure his pigeon didn't fly out the wrong hole. Merredith Jones gave him the briefest possible nod of recognition when their eyes met. She turned away as if she had seen something regrettable and sipped at her tea as if to get a bad taste out of her mouth.

LeRoy Stein was too self-involved to recognize Pasko or anyone else. He was wiping the bacon grease from his face with a stiff linen napkin, mumbling to himself. With an Italianate flourish, LeRoy signed the bill in the hope that at the end of the month Lettie would be generous and rip up his tab. Ever the dreamer, he told himself, getting into his Norfolk jacket with a bit of a struggle and catching sight of that garden-variety snake of a detective sitting at the bar. Pasko was doing a lousy job of feigning not to see him in the bar's gilded mirror and this clumsiness nearly endeared him to LeRoy.

LeRoy set his gentleman's circa 1952 beige Stetson on his head, just so, and left the hotel via the Main Street entry, pretending not to notice Pasko pretending not to notice him.

After being down in the dumps for he couldn't remember how long, LeRoy was suddenly feeling playful and bubbly. The day promised a sense of closure.

He was distracted from these thoughts when he caught a glimpse of Pasko gingerly stepping off the New Federal's porch, evidently tailing him.

This *was* fun, though one would think a man of Pasko's experience would be better at his job. It must have been easier following someone in New York, where Pasko received his early training, LeRoy decided. There, every newsstand, every bus shelter and subway entrance and stumblebum provided something to hide behind.

Here, there were mostly women, the ladies of the village going about Saturday morning chores and pleasures in durable spring pants suits. Not likely that Pasko could hide among them.

Even though the distance between the New Federal and Frank E. Taylor's Antiquarian Book Store was short, LeRoy managed to make long work of it, stopping every few feet to greet acquaintances. He fancied he could feel the negative energy of Pasko's frustration refracting off him.

Dolly Carlson, the owner/executive director of the Carlson B 'n' B, had acquired two Jack Russells, a fashionable breed of dog LeRoy held in contempt. Like buying a pet at Bergdorf's, he thought. Yet he managed to make a long fuss over the yapping bitches while Pasko dawdled in La Pizzeria's dank service alley.

There being no one else on Main Street with whom LeRoy cared to converse, he strolled into the otherwise empty Frank E. Taylor bookshop and had a few moments' literary intercourse with the gentleman owner while Pasko stewed outside.

Taylor, looking absurdly young for his age, recommended the new Mary Baker Eddy biography, but LeRoy said he didn't enjoy such sensational stuff and wanted to know what was hot in village mysteries. With contained disdain, Taylor directed him to the discreet mystery shelves at the rear of the shop.

Behind the mystery section, as LeRoy was aware,

were the bookstore's private facilities and, more importantly, its rear exit, which led to the parking lot.

By the time Pasko twigged to this, the parking lot was empty. A metal receiving door, which led into the rear of the watch factory and had supposedly been secured, was flapping in the mild spring breeze. The three "specials"—citizens hired at ten dollars a day and given minimal police powers in return for keeping watch over the various watch factory entries—were nowhere in sight.

Pasko began to run.

Chapter
27

WYN HAD BEEN REASSURED BY THE PROMISE OF THE "SPE-cials" Homer had hired out of his meager budget. The three of them, when not pursuing careers in the construction sector, were volunteer firemen along with Tommy in the village brigade. They were the embodiment of the manly American village volun-teer: genuinely idealistic under the beer bravado, strong and stalwart and capable of quick action and an enduring loyalty. Wyn conveniently discounted the remarks she had made in the past concerning their personal hygiene, intelligence quotients, and choice of female companionship.

As she unlocked the watch factory's impressive entry doors, she found herself thinking she wouldn't mind some genuine New York deli food right now, say a chicken-fat-laden chopped liver sandwich on rye with thin slices of Bermuda onion and a Dr. Brown's Cel-Ray tonic to help wash down the cholesterol. Figurative cold feet invariably made her yearn for what health nut Tommy considered poison.

"Do you want to die?" Tommy asked when last she wolfed down buttered popcorn at the movies.

"Eventually."

"It'll be a lousy death." He accompanied this pessimistic warning with such a concerned mortician's expression that Wyn had hugged him.

She put the golden glow of an outraged Tommy out of her mind, relieved as she entered the factory to find that the Village Cleaning Service had been reliable. The service bills were being footed by the Waggs Neck Savings and Loan, which now, thanks to the loan committee's idiotic and possibly criminal past judgment, owned the building.

But though the old, yellowed marble of the vaultlike entry foyer was free of dust and rodent droppings, there was a headache-inducing aroma of industrial pine disinfectant that recalled neglected ladies' facilities in rural gas stations.

Wyn, bemused by the vagaries her mind used to keep anxiety at bay, marched up the center of the dark stairwell, using the flashlight she congratulated herself for bringing. There hadn't been electricity in the factory for years. Shafts of daylight creeping through the iron shutters and the reinforced glass windows helped, but not immeasurably.

She opened the doors of the huge second-floor executive office and was sorry to see that their spring action still worked. They closed automatically, leaving her in the near dark, causing an otherworldly sound to emerge from somewhere within her. She refused to think that the murderer might have arrived first and was waiting for her in a corner, panty hose at the ready.

Using the dimming flashlight for illumination, Wyn

went to work on the windows, managing to get several open, though the heavy galvanized-iron storm shutters were more of a challenge.

In an attempt to keep her apprehension under control, she used her fear for strength as she contrived to pry one set of ancient, heavy shutters open. The clang they made as they swung up against the brick outer walls did nothing for her serenity.

The low tin-ceilinged room was now filled with the kind of shadowy half-light in which film noir directors liked to indulge. Wyn longed, at that moment, for convenience-store neon.

Disappointingly, the unobstructed window looked out on the New Federal's parking lot. Since there were no serviceable rear entries—all receiving doors had long been sealed—none of the specials had been posted in the lot. Wyn would have liked to be able to wave reassuringly to someone, to tip another conspirator the wink.

She felt as if it were three in the morning on Uranus and she was alone. She comforted herself with the belief that Homer and Pasko and half a dozen authentic policemen—reinforcements from West Sea—were waiting behind the doors that led into the handsome, deal-walled room.

Spacious as the room was, Wyn was beginning to feel claustrophobic; those low ceilings and blocked windows; that silent air of pretalkie doom. She half expected organ chords and Bela Lugosi in Dracula drag. She wished someone—even Bela—would come and end the suspense.

Pasko had disabused neither Wyn nor Homer of their belief in West Sea uniformed protection. These beliefs were based on his original proposal and not on Captain Savage's last-minute cut-rate changes.

"You're not going to tell her?" Cora asked that morning as Pasko got out of her pillow-rich bed and prepared to travel to Waggs Neck.

"Yeah, right, and put the kibosh on the whole deal." Strapping on his holster, he thought that Cora didn't look so bad in the morning and he probably was going to have to marry her. He had been saving money not using rubbers since their bargain: Cora would play personal computer jockey for him on this and any other case if he married her as soon as the Polish American Hall down in Riverhead had an opening. He told himself he had to look at this as a career move.

"If Little Miss Wet Dream gets strangled, you're not going to have much of a future in West Sea detection," Cora observed. She remembered the way Pasko had looked at Wyn and still didn't like it.

"That's cool. I'll stay home and take care of the kid." He didn't add, if there is a kid, not believing all that much in Cora's second announced pregnancy of the year.

"This time it's for real," Cora said, knowing what he was thinking.

"Yeah, yeah, like the color of your hair." He looked into her chorus girl eyes, wide with sincerity, and had a lingering doubt. "She's not getting strangled," Pasko said, returning to the subject of Wyn, giving Cora a kiss on her Kewpie doll forehead. "Trust me."

"Like all I got to do," Cora said, after he left, throwing aside the faux satin grass-green comforter, "is trust that conniving bastard."

Wyn's tummy was making unladylike noises. She knew that fear was her personal, internal Judas. Had she lived during the Inquisition, she would have betrayed friends, relatives, and sins with abandon, long before the toe clamps came out.

The dusted but stuffy room did not smell so much of pine disinfectant as of long-ago disappointments. Not to mention my own bouquet, Wyn thought; equal parts anxiety and panic. She wished she had spritzed more Fracas under her arms.

Her hands and forehead felt clammy and she had been in the building for only maybe a hot fifteen minutes. To distract herself, she moved to the far side of the room and managed to read the verdigrised bronze plaque above the fireplace: a memento mori honoring a young army officer killed in World War II. Martin Fiske, Myra's father, LeRoy's granddad.

Wyn wondered again if she was mistaken. If Pasko wasn't right. If, after all, LeRoy was the killer.

But then the double doors opened and Wyn turned, holding her moist palms together in an unconscious supplicant's gesture.

The client, better known as Merredith Jones, had arrived to keep her appointment.

Wyn, aware she had a regrettable propensity for self-congratulation, was surprised that she wasn't more exhilarated. She supposed there wasn't much glory in being right about events that were so wrong. She wished she had shared—how she disliked that social worker concept, sharing—her solution with someone. Homer, Pasko, Tommy, Liz.

Not that it mattered, she reassured herself. By this time Homer's specials had alerted the guns from West Sea to Merrie's presence in the building. By this time their ears were pressed up against the executive office doors, their tape recorders aglow and their trigger fingers itchy.

She wondered how much information she was going to have to elicit before they came in and announced Merrie was under arrest and read her her rights.

Merredith was smiling, revealing tiny, yellowish teeth that resembled good pearls in their lack of symmetry. Wyn found herself smiling back as if this were yet another social occasion between not quite peers.

Then she had to stifle a sudden urge to laugh, reminding herself this was serious business. But Merrie, in her bubble rain suit, looked like something out of an early television space series. Buck Rogers's mother. Dr. Video's spouse.

"Get it?" Merrie asked, as if they were already in midconversation, walking across the room with the surprising grace of an oversized boarding school girl who loved physical contact sports.

"I got it, Merrie," Wyn said, retreating behind the oak desk that had been too large and valueless to take away during the final desertion.

"Good." Merredith smiled as she ran her plastic ensconced finger along the edge of the desk, hunting for dust. "The funny thing is I got the idea of the panty hose from you. You don't remember, do you? You wore them to the closing when I bought Jones Junque for Frankie. I said how smart they were and you said they were the deal of the century and I should run right down to Bridgehampton and buy myself a dozen pair. As it happened, I took your advice."

"Does Frank know?"

"Frank doesn't want to know. Though of course I did it for him. He perked right up after the deaths of those two little schemers, McFee and Leverage. And he seemed to snap right out of another bad depression when Petro and that Carruthers person got theirs."

Merrie spread the panty hose out on the desk with

the loving care of a mother preparing the family wedding gown for her daughter. She folded the thin cardboard panel carefully, and placed it, again with precision, in one of her copious jacket pockets. "Neatness does count, don't you think?" she asked rhetorically as she gently stretched the panty hose legs with her plastic-gloved hands.

Holding the panty hose in front of her, Merrie came around the desk. Wyn felt her legs begin to shake. Ordering her feet not to desert her, she made her way round to the other side.

"My death would be pointless," Wyn said, moving to the far side of the desk as Merrie moved to the near.

"Why do you think that, dearie?"

"You were observed coming in. I expect the police will be breaking down the doors at any moment."

"Wyn, there was no one at the rear cargo door, which I undid last night. This morning I took the precaution of coming around the front where Homer's specials were having a high old time, smoking cigarettes and drinking beer, entertaining themselves, no doubt, with smutty stories."

Guessing that Merrie was about to try a lunge across the desk, Wyn decided enough was enough. She began to scream.

There was no response. She screamed again but the resoundingly empty echo wasn't reassuring.

"Told you. We're alone. If you struggle, it won't be neat but it might be more of a divertissement. Why don't you try a run for the doors?"

Wyn, losing it, succumbing to hysteria, did just that. She found herself being tackled several feet from her goal, the crotch of the panty hose up against her chin, Merrie sitting on her rump, carefully wrapping the panty hose legs around her neck.

Chapter
28

HOMER, UNCOMFORTABLY SEAT-BELTED INTO HIS WIFE'S TAURUS wagon, had been following Mike Bell on the traffic-laden Saturday morning Montauk Highway, for forty minutes. He had several unproductive and static-filled communications with Ray and Pasko and then his cell phone went dead.

Just as he was about to pull over and try to connect with Pasko and Ray via an old-fashioned pay phone, Mike Bell turned into an establishment heralded as East End Pre-Owned Motor Cars. The lot featured a number of ten-year-old Jaguars and Mercedes and the largest American flag Homer had ever seen.

Inside the minuscule and filthy office, Mike Bell and a forty-five-year-old fleshy fellow were trading punches with devil-may-care enthusiasm. Homer, who tried to break it up, heard a nasty cracking sound before he felt anything, having received a busted nose for his troubles.

Mike's opponent, not that Homer much cared, turned out to be the man who was dunning Mike for back payments on the Mustang.

Only after having his nose reset at the West Sea Hospital was Homer finally able to contact Pasko, and by then it was too late.

Ray Cardinal, in his blue and white Chevy truck, had followed Frank in his lipstick-red Porsche all the way up Swamp Road and onto the well-concealed dirt track known as Cheaters' Lane. At night, advanced village teenagers gathered here to engage in proscribed activities, evidenced by the number of empty Colt 45 cans and multicolored, ribbed, scented condoms littering the way.

Frank left the Porsche and marched through what the ecologists delight in calling wetlands. He sat on a decaying log and studied the swamp as if it held some answers. Tiny flying things buzzed around him. He was wearing jodhpurs and a fisherman's vest. His otherworldly good looks caused him to resemble a fairy tale book's woodland creature and made Ray Cardinal extra nervous.

"Want a cigarette?" Frank asked in his distinctive drawl.

"Don't smoke," Ray confessed, not knowing what action, if any, to take. Homer hadn't given him any other orders except to follow Frank Jones and cuff him if he tried to strangle Wyn Lewis.

Not knowing what else to do, Ray spit out his gum and sat on the far end of the log, increasingly uncomfortable with the flying bugs, stench of decay, and the tragic Frank Jones.

Tommy had been told—no, ordered—to butt out by everyone concerned. He had dutifully but unhappily gone to East Hampton and had spent one hour on the elaborate tree house his employer planned for her grandchildren—complete with electricity, cable capacity, and running water—before throwing down his pneumatic hammer and electric saw and deciding to butt in.

Speeding back to Waggs Neck, he saw Frank's Porsche careen down Swamp Road. Keeping up, just, was an out-of-uniform pink-faced Ray Cardinal in his souped-up Chevy truck.

Tommy kept driving, arriving at the watch factory in minutes, where he found his fire-fighting comrades sitting hilariously on the curb, having gone through most of a case of beer.

Across the street, LeRoy was strolling into the factory's front doors with his usual insouciance. This finally alerted the specials, who rose and were preparing to go after him when Pasko arrived and took charge.

Tommy was ahead of them, having parked his truck on the sidewalk, and sped up the staircase, two steps at a time. He tumbled into LeRoy, who had just opened the executive office doors and was trying to back out, believing he was interrupting an erotic encounter between Merrie and Wyn.

At that moment, the specials, led by an incendiary Pasko, came clambering up the steps.

Earlier, Pasko had lost LeRoy somewhere between the back door of the bookstore and the flapping receiving door of the watch factory. He was about to enter the factory when he looked back across the hotel parking lot and saw the rear door of La Pizzeria slamming shut. He had glimpsed the distinctive back belt of a Norfolk jacket, which he believed belonged to LeRoy.

Breathing hard, Pasko ran back across the parking lot

but found the pizza parlor's back door locked. He ran around and up the alley onto Main Street and into Mrs. Pizza. She was unlocking the glass and steel front door, still in her Norfolk car coat. "Where's Stein?" Pasko asked.

"Listen," Mrs. P. said, tiny tough hands on diminutive hips, "I just came in from the parking lot to open up and I'm the only one in here. What is this? Another example of the jack-booted fascist village regime, harassing innocent shop owners . . ."

Pasko ran back up the alley and across the hotel parking lot toward the watch factory, but the old receiving ramp door had swung shut, locking itself. In front of the building, Homer's specials were gathered, saying truthfully that they knew nothing.

Followed by the specials, Pasko ran up the dark stairs and into the open doors of the old executive office to find: LeRoy and Tommy attending Wyn, who was sitting on the oversized oak desk. She was taking great gulps of air, one hand to her neck in an old dowager gesture, as if reaching for her brooch. "Thanks for the protection," she managed to say in a whiskey voice that made her all the more attractive.

There was no answer to that so Pasko turned his attention to Merrie Jones.

She was standing at the open window facing the parking lot, wearing the look of a good loser. "I decided not to continue," she said in an even, logical voice, as if he asked, "so I threw in the towel. I mean I could hardly kill LeRoy and Tommy as well."

She rested both hands against the sides of the window. "Wyn, will you please tell Frank this was the only choice. How could I be in Sing Sing—or wherever they'd put me—while he was in Waggs Neck Harbor?

I would be miserable and so would he. My way sets us both free."

This was when Pasko made a move to reach her, but Merrie, with the grace of her innate athleticism, leaped through the window into the sunshine to the brick parking lot below.

There followed an inhuman sound that paralyzed everyone in the room. Pasko was the first to recover and the first to reach Merrie. The village considered it only right that she died of a broken neck.

Chapter
29

IT WAS SATURDAY, MAY 1, A FULLY DEVELOPED KODACOLOR
spring day, purple lilacs and local ladies in luscious,
odoriferous bloom. The New Federal Inn Centennial
Celebration parade was in full swing, half the populace
marching in festive footwear or riding in appropriate
vehicles down a patriotically decorated Main Street.

Yo Yo, the Japanese restaurant, had its windows
wrapped in red, white, and blue boys' kites. The Eden
Café had outdone itself with row after row of initialed
blueberry and cranberry muffins arranged in such a
way that "New Federal Inn" was spelled out.

Dickie ffrench, appalled by these efforts, created a
simple, dignified, and irrelevant exhibit by placing in
the main display window of ffrench's Fine Antiques a
portrait of the Father of Our County. An earlyish American flag was waving enthusiastically, thanks to a hidden electric fan.

Dignitaries in the trembling reviewing stands

placed in front of the Municipal Building—draped in the Republic's colors—held up their end, pretending an interest in the various school bands that few of them felt.

Mike Bell, former general manager of the New Federal, was not pretending. He was taking shelter from the parade at the bar of the Blue Buoy Bar & Grill. Sitting next to him on a worn stool was the Junoesque Heidi Lum, sipping at a rum and Coke. They were observing her eighteenth birthday ("Now I'm legal," she announced to her mother's dismay) and Mike's passing the New York State Real Estate Boards.

Heidi's mum, Liz Lum, a nervous test taker, had failed by two miserable points on this, her second attempt. "It was the closing statement that did me in," Liz said. "Next time I'll really bone up on the math."

Mike Bell had had the *chutzpah* to ask Wyn for a job as a real estate salesman, disregarding the fact that Wyn had said long ago that she would never hire a Bell to work for her in any capacity.

Wyn had become more diplomatic with the passing years and had developed a belief that one should encourage any ambition whatsoever in a Bell. Thus she suggested Mike work for West Sea Realty for a year or so and acquire seasoning.

"Scared I'll take away some of your action?" Mike had asked, offended.

"No, I'm afraid you'll turn off all the clients with your attitude," Wyn returned, having come to the end of her patience.

He had been fired from his New Federal position when Lettie returned to his room one midmorning to retrieve an earring and found Heidi and Mike in acrobatic flagrante delicto. "And that's being kind," Lettie

said to Wyn, whose shoulder she had come to cry upon.
"After all I did for that gorilla . . ."

Luckily, the Centennial held her interest, and LeRoy
Stein was developing into a sterling hotel general manager, knowing when to grovel and when to be snide.
Besides, he was an amusing companion, Lettie allowed,
though—and this was perhaps all to the good—not in
bed.

After the parade, the street-floor public rooms of the
New Federal were opened to the hoi polloi and lemon-
ade and store-bought cookies were served.

The more exclusive luncheon gathering up at the
Rooftop Café was given by Lettitia Browne for, as she
put it, "all the marvelous Waggs Neck Harborites who
have contributed to the legend that is the New Federal Inn."

Lettie was wearing a taxicab yellow Galanos sheath
with a breezy hat to match. Dickie, in a white ice cream
suit and bow tie, thought she looked very Margaret
Truman, circa 1948, about to launch a ship. Lettie said
he did, too.

Pasko had to move around Dickie and Lettie to get
to his spouse. He had had to marry Cora earlier than
planned in order to keep her old-fashioned family from
appearing at his door with a shotgun.

Noticeably pregnant almost from week one, Cora was
thrilled to be invited to what she told her mother was
the Waggs Neck Harbor social event of the year.

Cora had already proved to be an effective helpmate.
She had sent anonymous but official-looking faxes to
everyone she could think of, most especially the senator
and his aides and the local press. These communications carried the news that Captain Savage had put a
citizen's (Wyn's) life in danger by a foolish, pennywise
decision. His stratagem, according to the fax, would

have had tragic consequences if it weren't for Lieutenant Detective Pasko.

The result of an inquiry sparked by the fax ended in Captain Savage's early retirement. The hero of the moment, Pasko, was promoted to take his place.

At the West Sea ceremony in which this event was recorded by the local media (the senator was the proud award giver), Pasko allowed himself an appalling insight: He was never going to return to the NYPD. In less than a month he had become everything he hadn't wanted to be: a bureaucrat, a husband, an expectant father, and the owner of a heavily mortgaged cottage in Waggs Neck Harbor village.

This handyman's special had been sold with the connivance of Cora and, as a song of his teenage years once suggested, a "devil in angel's disguise."

The devil and Tommy and an entire contingent of Waggs Neck Harborites had turned up in West Sea for the awards parade. Homer received an award as well as equal attention, the senator going after both the liberal and the East End black vote in his usual pull-out-all-the-stops style. "A sterling example," he told an *East Hampton Star* reporter, "of the black and white law enforcement communities working as one."

As Pasko stood alone for a moment in front of the melancholy crime fighter's building, medal in hand, he watched Wyn and Tommy get into her Jaguar. He felt as unhappy as he ever had, for he knew, without a doubt, that he had lost not only his chance at New York but his shot at Wyn as well.

"Every woman in the village seems to be pregnant or a recent mother except you and me," said Liz Lum, sticking long foot in large mouth, as a maternity-dress-clad Cora Pasko walked by, intent on kissing Lettie Browne's hand, determined to be a power in village society.

"Yeah," Tommy said, putting his hand on Wyn's shoulder.

Wyn hoped this was a gesture of reassurance signifying that Tommy would love her anyway, even if she was an aging, barren Realtor.

After an elegant buffet focused on thin, white, tinned asparagus and medallions of frozen chicken, waiters passed around one plastic glass of New York champagne to each of the invitees. Lettie stood up, called for silence, and gave her famous Madame-Curie-accepting-the-Nobel-prize speech she had delivered in her last television outing. The performance would have been especially moving if nearly everyone hadn't heard it before. What it had to do with the hundredth anniversary of the founding of the New Federal was anybody's guess.

It was as the assemblage was downing their champagne that Wyn had an admittedly hokey, abysmal, and contrary change of heart. She suddenly felt that she wanted to leave more behind than record sales of tricked-up bungaloids and restored gingerbreaded cottages.

She caught sight of Pasko, wrist clasped by Cora in the style of a police guard escorting a prisoner to penitentiary, and decided that she might be wrong but enforced intimacy was better than no intimacy at all.

She turned to Tommy and brought his adorable stickout boy's ear to her lips and said, " 'Barkis is willin'.' "

"You said that before when you agreed to marry me. Dickens. I looked it up."

"How enterprising."

He kissed her very deliberately on the lips and for a moment they were transported to that special world they inhabited and no one who knew either of them could hope to understand.

When they arrived back from their quick trip to the moon on gossamer wings, Lettie was just winding up, Tommy was wearing an extremely irritating self-congratulatory grin, and Wyn felt motherhood and a new kind of intimacy looming.

Epilogue

CLEARLY HE WAS SOMEONE. NO ONE LOOKED LIKE THAT AND wasn't *someone*. The drop-dead chic cosmopolitan crowd in the Manhattan hotel's Philippe Starck-designed restaurant recognized his celebrity without being able to pinpoint it. It was driving them nuts. Who the hell *was* he?

The blue shadings under his copper-colored eyes made him a bit too jaded to be a Calvin Klein model. He might have been one of the new movie stars, all spare and spiffy in his collarless Italian suit, but the beautiful, tortured face was more reminiscent of Montgomery Clift than Keanu Reeves and besides, he was too comfortable with himself to be an actor.

Wyn stood at the maître d'hôtel's white podium for a moment, dreadfully aware that she was the only woman in the place whose anorexia was not wrapped in stark white or widow black. Deciding she didn't care, she followed the penguinesque headwaiter to Frank Jones's table.

Frank told her she was looking especially gorgeous

and alive and she said ditto, though he didn't look too alive to her. He waved away the handwritten menu but Wyn studied it with care, choosing a vegetarian lasagna because Tommy would want her to. She was getting sentimental in her old age.

"Meeting with your mother a pleasant event?" Frank asked, nonchalantly.

" 'Pleasant event' is a euphemism for what goes on between my mother and me. She complained bitterly about my nails, hair, and eating habits. I told her I was with child and she reacted with a 'How nice for you, dear' dismissal of the subject."

The penguin disguised as a headwaiter appeared and said a gentleman wanted to send them a bottle of wine and what kind would they like. Frank said to be sure and say thank you but neither of them drank other people's wines. He took a gulp of his Mondavi as if it were a soft drink and smiled at Wyn.

"Merrie left me tons of money. So I'm rich, I'm nice to look at, and my mental health seems to have been miraculously stabilized thanks to new drugs and a whiz of a shrink who charges two hundred dollars a fifty-minute hour. I wonder how long I'm going to live to enjoy all that."

"Forever," Wyn said, not liking the turn this talk was taking, wishing she had something other than strawberry-flavored designer water in her glass. Tommy would have a cow if she ordered a carbonated beverage or wine, or what she wanted most, a pink gin. Not that she had ever had a pink gin but the atmosphere of the restaurant called for it.

"You brought the papers," Frank said rather than asked.

Wyn said that Realtors never forgot. She removed the contracts from the cutting-edge rubber-and-nylon briefcase LeRoy had given her as a replacement for her old, politically incorrect leather one. She watched as Frank signed the documents that gave Wyn the exclusive right to market all of his Waggs Neck village properties with the exception of Jones Junque. He had deeded it over to Art in Public Environments (APE) along with an annual grant to maintain it.

"It's time, don't you think?" Frank asked, referring to the unburdening of his portfolio of real estate investments, looking at Wyn as if he really wanted an answer.

"Long past." The lasagna arrived and Wyn tucked in with her usual gusto. "What are you going to do?" she asked as Frank watched her eat her way through it.

"I'm not sure. 'Too many options,' said the little prince who couldn't smile. Right now I'm leaning toward going back to school, getting a masters in social work and maybe even a doctorate. I might end up working with disturbed kids. Actually, they call them disadvantaged kids now. Jesus and Mary know I've had mucho experience." The little prince finally did smile but it wasn't one that reached his eyes.

"There's all that money. Even after the estate taxes there are gazillions. Merrie once said real money brings with it an awesome responsibility and she was right. One part of me wants to buy a yacht and a blazer and a bevy of chorus girls . . . but I think it's too late to join the old international set. I'm going to save a mad-cap existence for another life.

"In the meanwhile, I'm trying to be careful. The only major commitment I've made thus far is to set up the Merredith Jones Trust at the Henry Street Settlement. It establishes a private high school for kids who can't make it in public ones."

Wyn said that was an admirable thing to do and then waited. The paperwork could easily have been done via

FedEx and though this Manhattan meeting serendipitously coincided with the one with her mother, Frank had evidently set it up because he had more to say. After a few moments, he did so. "You want to do me a favor?" he asked, after the lasagna plate was dispatched.

"I never answer that question," Wyn admitted, "before knowing what the favor is. Certainly, in the great scheme of things, Frank, I'd love to do you a favor."

"Good. Let's get out of here and go back to the apartment. I'm ready to talk about it."

But am I ready to listen? Wyn asked herself as she gathered up her briefcase and followed him along with the eyes of half the room.

The apartment was huge and stuffy and on the top of a comfortless Fifth Avenue apartment house noted for the quiet social prestige of its long-time denizens. Frank was attractively out of place, like a figure in a Joseph Cornell construction meant to disorient: Contemporary Man in a *Fin de Siècle* Setting.

The congenial fellow in the casual servant's outfit who had let them in brought tea neither of them wanted and set it on an oversized mahogany table in the overfurnished living room. The heavy drapes had been pulled back but the resultant panoramic view of a late autumn Central Park provided no cheer.

"You go first," Wyn said from the depths of a cut velvet-upholstered armchair reminiscent of the sofa in her house in Waggs Neck, which seemed oh, a thousand miles removed.

"Fine," Frank said, pouring the scented green tea into thin cups, mostly for something to do. "I knew from the beginning but I didn't exactly *want* to know, if you know what I mean," he said, getting right into it, evoking Merrie and her jump-to-the-chase conversations. "Penny's and Harriet's deaths were too convenient. Not that they get much sympathy from me. Between them they ruined my father and Myra, conning them into buying the duck farm from the Bells when they had neither the expertise nor the capital to develop it.

"I wonder how many crooked permits the McFee-Leverage Co. girls cooked up between them; they had such a tidy racket. Penny, vedy Southampton, sitting on any number of pro bono boards, including, of course, the zoning board; Harriet, much more 'of the people,' presenting herself as a dedicated environmentalist.

"Regarding the duck farm deal, they made the big mistake of wanting more money, *after* they had killed the Bells' business, scammed Myra and my dad, and then sold it to Merrie. Merrie had paid once and she wasn't going to pay again. It wasn't sportsmanly. Merrie killed them in the name of fairness.

"I wanted to leave her then but it wasn't possible. I was afraid of her in a way."

"Afraid of her," Wyn repeated. "Why we all thought you and she . . ."

"I know. But I was the only person Merrie had ever loved in her life. When I was born, she immediately became the little mother. My birth gave her a role. When they sent her away to live with our aunt, she thought she would die. I had Myra Stein in my life. Merrie had no one but me. I felt an obligation to return her affection and loyalty."

"Didn't Flinty object to Merrie being taken off like that?"

"He was relieved. He never thought of her as his. She belonged to the Hollidays. I was his.

"Until Merrie decided it was time to come back into

my life. She had a solid sense of her own logic—of what was right and what was wrong according to her own book of rules. She would never have let me go even if I had wanted to; she had been so loyal. Nor could she conceive of me as a separate being; after a time, neither could I. She told me she had dedicated her life to me. What was fair, she often said, was fair."

"I'm still not clear if you knew about her tiny propensity for strangling real estate brokers," Wyn said.

"You're not unlike her." Frank unfolded himself and moved to the windows, the waning New York sun backlighting him theatrically. "Relentless logic. *I* don't know if I knew, Wyn; I said that already. I wouldn't allow myself to know. I don't suppose I could."

"What about Petro and Kathy?" Wyn asked, putting a cube of sugar in her tea, silently telling Tommy what he could do with his health strictures. Cubes of sugar in a private house were a minor luxury, one in which she meant to indulge.

"I'm a master at self-delusion, but even so it was difficult not to know that Merrie had gotten rid of those wretched women. Both murders had all the earmarks of Merrie righting what she saw as a breaking of the rules.

"I was at lunch when Petro and Kathy Carruthers asked Merrie to buy up their shares of the duck farm corporation for big-time money. They had cast Merrie as their walking, talking retirement fund. In exchange, they promised to never mention that they had gotten the zoning board to outlaw the duck farm and had secured the variances that eventually allowed Merrie to develop that upscale Levittown.

"Merrie said it wasn't fair that those two bitches, who had conned Myra and Flinty into buying what they couldn't afford, should now be bleeding us for the

224

money we made on that same property. They had set us all up and one had to agree with Merrie."

"So," Wyn said, "she killed them."

"When I realized what she had done, I withdrew. But I guessed you were going to be next. Merrie had taken it into her head that all the Realtors involved in those long-ago deals were in cahoots and you were as well. After all, Merrie said, Wyn Lewis is the only one among them with real brains."

"I'm flattered, I think. So you were the one who wrapped the panty hose around my steering wheel?"

"I wanted to warn you."

Wyn, suddenly tired of the Old New York atmosphere and Frank's frail what-could-I-do defense, stood up. "You should have warned a few other people earlier, Frank. Petro and Kathy weren't simon-pure but they didn't deserve to be killed."

Wyn paused and then, thinking she'd probably never get this opportunity again, decided to say it all. "Merrie said she did it for you. She strangled those women for your mental well-being."

When Frank didn't comment, Wyn said, "Think of their terror, Frank."

"I do. Every moment of every day."

The private elevator arrived and Wyn stepped into it feeling as if she were being liberated from someone else's hell. She left Frank in that dead apartment and headed for Penn Station and home and her lifeline.